A. J. ASH

The Bond That Waited

First edition

This book was professionally typeset on Reedsy.
Find out more at reedsy.com

Contents

Trigger Warnings

Content Notice

This novel contains themes that may be distressing for some readers.

Content warnings include:

- Violence and threat of violence
- Blood, blood exchange, and feeding
- Exile, social rejection, and abandonment
- Emotional trauma
- Power imbalance and political manipulation
- Explicit sexual content
- Sexual content involving altered states or magical influence
- Reproductive coercion themes
- Fertility manipulation
- Death threats and attempted murder

This story is intended for mature audiences and explores dark fantasy themes alongside romance.

Reader discretion is advised.

Your well-being matters. Please take care while reading.

One

Rowan

The night the pack shifted, I tied my hair back and stood alone.

Dark strands slid through my fingers as I twisted them into a tight ponytail, the motion automatic. Long hair was a liability. Anything that caught, snagged, or distracted had no place in the field.

Around me, clothes were shed without ceremony. Bodies moved into position beneath the open sky, bare skin already braced for the change. I folded my clothes at the edge of the clearing and stepped into the grass.

I was tall enough to feel exposed even among the others. Five foot nine, shoulders squared, posture straight. I did not shrink. I never had.

The moon hung low and pale above us.

The shift came fast for everyone else.

Fur tore through skin in sharp, wet sounds I had heard my entire life. Bones cracked and reformed. Breath broke into snarls and growls as bodies bent to the moon's call. Power rolled across the clearing, heavy and unmistakable.

I closed my eyes and drew in a breath.

I had done this before. Every cycle.

Nothing happened.

I opened my eyes. Wolves stood where people had been moments earlier—massive shapes shaking out their fur as if the transformation were nothing more than a stretch. Some looked away. Others didn't bother.

The pause followed.

Then understanding.

Heat burned behind my eyes. My chest tightened, pressure building against something that refused to give.

Not to the moon, I thought. Inward.

My wolf answered immediately.

Not weak. Not silent.

She pressed against me, furious and contained, coiled tight beneath my ribs.

Not yet, she warned.

I stood naked in the clearing while my body remained stubbornly human.

A short laugh cut through the quiet.

That was enough.

I turned and ran.

I didn't stumble. I didn't hesitate. I ran the way I'd been taught, head down, stride steady, even as tears blurred my vision. Grass tore at my feet. The night swallowed me.

I didn't stop until my lungs burned.

When I collapsed against a tree, I wrapped my arms around myself and shook. I hated crying. It felt uncontrolled. Useless. The sound tore out of me anyway, rough and quiet.

My wolf pressed close, incandescent with rage.

I am here, she promised.

"I know," I whispered. It was the only thing holding me together.

When I returned to the pack grounds, I was dressed and silent. No one spoke to me. No one needed to.

Ash Valley noticed everything. Especially failure.

The Alpha stood at the center of the clearing, human again. Calm. Unyielding. His gaze found me and lingered just long enough to strip away hope.

"Rowan," he said. "Step forward."

I did.

"You failed to shift," he said. "Again."

The murmurs were low. Controlled.

"You will stand before the council tomorrow. Your place in Ash Valley will be decided then."

A failure of a wolf.

My wolf surged against me, furious and restrained, her need to protect clashing with the force that held her still.

Two halves of a whole.

I lifted my chin and met the Alpha's gaze. I would not beg. I would not perform softness for them.

Ash Valley was strong.

Tomorrow, they would decide whether strength was something I was allowed to be.

Two

Rowan

The council chamber smelled like stone and ash.

It always did. Old rock. Old rules. The kind of place where decisions were made slowly and never undone. I stood in the center of the circle with my hands at my sides, spine straight, hair pulled back tight the way I wore it when I needed to be steady.

The elders sat first. The Alpha stood behind them.

Tristen did not look at me when I entered.

That told me everything.

Ash Valley did not hold trials to seek truth. It held them to confirm conclusions already reached.

"You stand before the council," one of the elders began, voice dry and practiced, "to answer for your failure to shift."

Failure.

The word landed clean and sharp. No embellishment. No apology.

"I have trained," I said. "I have followed every directive given to me."

No one interrupted. That was not courtesy. It was indifference.

"Results matter more than effort," another elder replied. "You know this."

Tristen finally met my gaze. His expression was calm, controlled, carved into certainty. He had been a strong Alpha. Ash Valley had thrived under him.

That was the part of this that cut deepest.

He believed he was right.

"You have reached the final threshold," he said. "There will be no further allowances."

A murmur rippled through the chamber. Not surprise. Expectation.

"You are a risk," Tristen continued. "To yourself and to the pack."

My wolf stirred, anger flashing hot and sharp, but she did not act. Still, she waited.

"What is your judgment?" an elder asked.

Tristen did not hesitate.

"Exile."

The word echoed once, then settled.

"You will leave Ash Valley," he said. "You have two hours to gather what you will carry. You are not to return. If you cross our borders again, you will be treated as a threat."

A lone wolf.

I nodded once. It was the only response I trusted myself to give.

"Two hours," Tristen repeated. "Then the boundary will close to you." His gaze hardened.

"You are exiled," he said. "And you will remain unaligned."

That landed heavier than the sentence itself.

No one stepped forward.

Not a mentor. Not a training partner. Not a single voice raised in objection.

I had been pack-raised, not pack-born. An orphan taken in because Ash Valley did not abandon children—only adults who failed to become what they were meant to be.

They had fed me. Trained me. Sharpened me.

And when I did not shift, they called it betrayal.

I lifted my chin anyway.

"You will not seek shelter with another pack," Tristen continued. "You will not swear loyalty elsewhere. If you bind yourself to another territory or align with another Alpha, Ash Valley will consider it treason."

A quiet murmur rippled through the chamber.

"And treason," he finished calmly, "will be answered with death."

My wolf snarled, pressing hard against my ribs, but I did not move. Did not speak.

Alone was permitted.

Belonging was not.

I turned and walked out without waiting to be dismissed.

No one stopped me.

I packed quickly.

Clothes. Boots. A knife I had earned during training. A small pouch of supplies. Nothing sentimental. Ash Valley had never allowed room for that.

When I stepped beyond the last marker stone, the air changed.

The boundary burned.

Not heat—pressure. A sudden, vicious sensation that tore through my chest and down my spine, stealing the breath from my lungs. I stumbled, clutching at myself as something unseen ripped away.

My bond to the pack.

It felt like skin being peeled back. Like a thread snapping that I hadn't known was there until it was gone. My wolf cried out inside me, rage and grief tangled tight.

Then silence.

Not hers.

The pack's.

I dropped to one knee, gasping, hands pressed into the dirt. When the pain eased, the world felt larger. Emptier.

I was packless.

I stood slowly and did not look back.

I walked for days.

It felt like weeks because I never stopped listening for pursuit. I slowed deliberately. Changed direction. Waited in places that would give me warning. If they were coming, I wanted to know.

They never did.

In truth, it was four—maybe five—days on foot.

I ate what the forest allowed. Roots, berries, small game when I could catch it. My wolf guided me to safe water, to sheltered ground, to places that would not scent me too strongly.

Sleep never came.

I rested in short, restless stretches, eyes open, body ready. Even when exhaustion dragged at my bones, I kept moving.

By the time the land changed, I felt hollowed out.

When I crossed into unfamiliar territory, there was no burn.

No warning.

No rejection.

Just a subtle shift in the air—heavy, watchful, old.

I didn't know whose land I had entered.

Only that my wolf lifted her head for the first time since exile.

Alert.

Aware.

Waiting.

The nights were the worst.

Not because I was alone—but because I wasn't allowed not to be.

Ash Valley had made that clear.

Survival was acceptable.

Belonging was not.

And if they ever scented another pack on me—if I ever let myself align again—they would come.

Three

Ciaran

The patrol returned at dawn.

Maeve was with them, cloak dusted with ash, her expression sharp with interest rather than concern. That alone was unusual.

"They found a wolf," she said as soon as she entered the hall.

I paused mid-step. "In our territory?"

"Yes. Alive. Alone."

That was worse.

A lone wolf crossing the border warranted attention. One without pack marks warranted consequence.

I closed my eyes briefly and extended my awareness into the land itself.

The territory did not recoil.

It did not recognize her as a threat.

She had crossed the boundary exhausted. Unshielded. Barely holding herself together.

Not hunting.

Surviving.

The certainty settled deep and immediate. Whatever had entered my lands meant no harm.

"And yet," Maeve said lightly, watching me. "You feel it."

I opened my eyes. "Where?"

"Near the eastern boundary. No aggression. No pack scent."

There it was again—that subtle pull brushing my awareness like a question waiting to be answered.

I did not react.

"Do you want her detained," Maeve asked, "or brought to you?"

I considered the implications. Vampire law allowed containment. It discouraged cruelty. A wolf in our territory would be noticed.

"No," I said at last. "Do not arrest her."

Maeve's brow lifted. She knew me well enough to hear what I wasn't saying.

"I will go," I added. "Alone."

Her smile was slow. Knowing. "I thought you might."

The eastern boundary was quiet.

I moved through the trees without haste, cloak drawn back, boots silent against the forest floor. Dawn light filtered pale and cold through the branches.

The pull strengthened as I went.

Not hunger.

Recognition.

I slowed as the air shifted ahead. There was a presence there—human-shaped, wolf-scented, wary but not hostile.

Alone.

I stepped into the clearing and stopped.

She stood near the trees, posture squared despite exhaustion that clung to her like a second skin. Tall for a wolf. Dark hair pulled back. Travel-worn clothes. Scuffed boots.

The bond snapped into focus.

Not sealed. Not awakened.

But undeniably there.

The weight of it settled into my chest, sharp enough to steal my breath for a single, unguarded moment. I had felt it before—distant, unfinished.

Now it stood in front of me.

Attraction followed, swift and dangerous.

Not lust.

Awareness sharpened into something immediate and undeniable. My instincts leaned forward even as my body remained still.

She should have looked fragile.

She did not.

Her gaze snapped to me at once. No fear. No challenge.

Assessment.

Good.

I buried the reaction before it could surface. Did not reach for power. Did not let the bond stir visibly between us. Wolves who had already lost everything did not respond well to pressure.

I would not be another force that tried to take.

"You've crossed into vampire territory," I said evenly. "Do you know where you are?"

Her jaw tightened. "No. I wasn't tracking borders."

"You are alone."

Resolve flickered through her eyes. "I am."

The bond surged again. I held it down without effort.

"You are not under arrest," I said. "But you are within my lands. That makes you my responsibility."

Her shoulders eased—not trust. Calculation.

"I don't want trouble."

"I know."

She studied me openly now, gaze lingering just long enough to note the absence of threat.

"What happens now?"

The answer would ripple outward into courts and packs and futures already shifting.

"For now," I said, "you come with me."

"And if I refuse?"

"I will not force you," I replied. "But the world beyond these trees is not safe for a lone wolf."

She held my gaze, choice moving behind her eyes.

"Fine," she said. "For now."

That was enough.

I turned, trusting she would follow.

Behind me, her steps fell into alignment with my path, the bond between us stirring quietly.

Waiting.

Four

Ciaran

The path back to the castle curved through dense forest before opening onto a stone-laid road. I kept my pace measured. Far enough ahead that she did not feel her back pressed against my presence. Close enough to intervene if needed.

She followed without complaint.

That alone told me more than most words would have.

Wolves accustomed to authority often bristled under silence. She did not. She walked as someone used to deciding when to speak and when not to. Her movements were efficient. Balanced. Even exhausted, she wasted nothing.

The pull was constant now. Not insistent. Just present—a quiet pressure at the center of my chest that sharpened when she drew closer, softened when she drifted away.

I did not let it show.

"What were you doing near the border?" I asked after a time.

She glanced at me briefly. "Traveling."

"That is not an answer."

"It is the honest one."

"You do not move like someone running blindly."

"No," she said. "I move like someone who intends to stay alive."

A smile surfaced before I could stop it. Small. Controlled.

She noticed.

Her gaze flicked toward me, assessing. Curious. Alert in the way of someone who had learned caution early.

I looked away first.

I should not have been aware of the line of her neck, the steady strength in her stride, the way her scent shifted when she relaxed.

I was.

I acknowledged it and set it aside.

"How long have you been alone?" I asked.

Her jaw tightened. Just slightly.

"Long enough."

Not evasion. A boundary.

I respected it.

"You crossed into vampire land without realizing it," I said. "That tells me you have not traveled here before."

"No," she replied. "I did not intend to."

"Intention matters," I said. "But so does circumstance."

She gave a quiet laugh. Not amused. More acknowledgment than humor.

"You sound like someone who has had to explain consequences before."

"Frequently."

Silence stretched again, easy in a way that surprised me.

"What should I call you?" she asked suddenly.

The question landed softly—and changed everything.

Names mattered. More than most creatures realized. They were invitations. Anchors. Claims, if offered carelessly.

I considered her as I answered.

"Ciaran," I said at last.

It was true. And not.

Her brows drew together slightly, instinct catching on the omission. She did not press.

"And you?" I asked.

"Rowan."

The bond stirred at the sound of it. Subtle. Attentive.

I kept my expression neutral.

"You do not have to stay," I said, returning us to safer ground. "Once we reach the castle, you will be offered options."

Her pace slowed. "Options usually come with expectations."

"They do," I agreed. "But not obligations."

She studied me openly then. I let her. Better she see what I was than imagine something worse.

Tall. Still. Controlled. No display of power.

Her gaze dipped once before returning to my face.

I felt the reaction and contained it without effort.

"You do not behave like other vampires," she said.

"No," I replied. "I do not."

She nodded, as if confirming something for herself.

Silence settled between us again. Not strained. Not empty.

With each step closer to the castle, the restraint I carried tightened—not from struggle, but from intent.

There would be time.

There would be choice.

When the bond was accepted—when it was *opened*—I would give her something no one else ever had.

Not a title.

Not a claim.

A name meant only for us.

Roe.

The thought settled deep and dangerous, and I locked it away.

Until then, control was not just preference.

It was protection.

Five

Rowan

We walked on in silence after that.

Something had shifted, subtle but undeniable, and I didn't yet have the words for it. Knowing his name changed the shape of my thoughts in a way that unsettled me.

Ciaran.

It lingered in my mind longer than it should have.

I should have been paying attention to where we were going.

Instead, I was aware of him.

He moved with unhurried confidence, long strides eating up the path as if the land yielded to him by habit. Tall. Broad-shouldered beneath dark fabric. Black hair loose at his neck.

It was distracting.

Annoyingly so.

I clenched my hands and fixed my gaze on the stonework beneath my boots. That lasted only a moment before my attention drifted again.

My wolf stirred, amused.

You are paying attention.

"I don't have a choice," I thought back.

You always do.

That wasn't helpful.

There was something about him that pressed at my awareness—a steady hum beneath my skin that had nothing to do with fear. His presence filled the space without crowding it, restrained in a way that felt deliberate.

It made my instincts lean forward even as my reason pulled back.

I was barely twenty. Ash Valley had not encouraged indulgence. Survival came first. Strength second. Everything else was unnecessary.

And yet my attention kept circling back to him.

My wolf pressed closer, curious rather than alarmed.

He is careful, she observed.

"That doesn't make him safe," I replied internally.

No, she agreed. *But it makes him interesting.*

I drew in a slow breath and forced my focus outward.

The forest thinned as the path widened, stonework emerging beneath my feet. Ahead, the castle rose from the land itself—dark, imposing, carved rather than built. Ancient. Controlled.

Dangerous in a quiet way.

Like him.

Ciaran glanced back once, and our eyes met.

Awareness sparked—sharp, immediate.

I broke eye contact first, jaw tightening as I refocused on walking.

Control, my wolf murmured. *You have learned that.*

"Not enough," I muttered.

He adjusted his pace to match mine without crowding my space. I became acutely aware of the difference in our heights, the restraint in his movements, the way he did not look at me for too long.

As if he were holding something back.

That realization sent a brief, unwelcome shiver through me.

Whatever this was—whatever my wolf sensed and my body reacted to—I would deal with it later.

Right now, survival still came first.

Even if my instincts disagreed.

Six

Rowan

The castle was quieter at night than I expected.

Stone corridors swallowed sound, torchlight flickering low along the walls as Ciaran led me through a series of turns that felt intentional without being disorienting. Nothing here was meant to overwhelm.

Everything had a purpose.

Including me.

We stopped outside a smaller sitting room set back from the main hall. Firelight spilled through the open doorway, warm and steady, carrying the faint scent of herbs and dried citrus.

Maeve was already inside.

She rose as we entered, her attention fixing on me immediately. Not predatory. Not assessing rank. Curious in a way that felt sharp without being unkind.

"So," she said lightly. "This must be the wolf."

"I have a name," I replied before I could stop myself.

Her mouth curved. "Good. That means you'll insist on using it."

She crossed the room and offered her hand. I hesitated only a moment before taking it.

"Maeve," she said. "Welcome."

Her grip was firm—steady, equal. No testing.

"Rowan."

Something flickered behind her eyes. Recognition. Confirmation.

Ciaran watched the exchange without comment.

Maeve moved back toward the table and began pouring tea from a ceramic pot, the liquid steaming as it filled three cups. She handed one to me without asking.

"Drink," she said. "It helps settle nerves."

I accepted it cautiously. The taste was mint and something floral I didn't recognize.

Ciaran did not take a cup.

Instead, he crossed to the sideboard and poured himself a glass of amber liquid from a cut-crystal decanter. The scent was sharp and warm and nothing like the tea.

I watched him take a slow swallow.

Then I looked down at my cup.

"Can I have that instead?" I asked, nodding toward his glass.

Ciaran paused.

"No," he said calmly. "You should have the tea."

I met his gaze. "I don't like being managed."

That earned a look from Maeve. Amused. Interested.

After a moment, Ciaran sighed—not in irritation, but resignation—and set the decanter back down.

"One," he said. "And slowly."

I took the glass from him without arguing.

The liquor burned on the way down, rich and warming, settling low in my chest in a way the tea hadn't.

Maeve settled into her chair, watching us both.

"You are not under arrest," she said plainly. "You are not a prisoner. And you are not obligated to stay."

That earned my full attention.

"You have choices," Ciaran added. "Three."

Maeve lifted a finger. "First. You leave tonight. We'll escort you to the border."

A second finger. "Second. You stay as a guest. Temporary. No expectations."

She glanced briefly at Ciaran before continuing.

"And third—you remain under the Prince's protection."

The word landed before I could stop it.

Prince.

I looked at Ciaran.

He did not correct her.

Maeve's eyes widened just a fraction. "Ah. That wasn't meant to be said yet."

Silence pressed in.

Ciaran's jaw tightened—not with anger, but with calculation.

"Well," Maeve continued smoothly, standing, "now that's done."

She drained her tea and turned toward the door, then paused as if listening to something I couldn't hear.

A beat.

Then another.

"Of course," she said quietly.

She looked back at us. "I'm being summoned. Try not to kill each other while I'm gone."

And then she was gone, the door closing softly behind her.

The room felt different without her.

He remained standing where he was, posture relaxed but alert.

"Do you want more tea?" he asked.

I lifted his glass instead. "No."

He opened his mouth to argue.

I took another swallow.

The warmth spread faster this time.

Ciaran exhaled slowly and refilled the glass without comment.

I wrapped my hands around it, grounding myself.

"I don't decide well when I feel cornered," I said.

"You are not cornered," he replied. "You are choosing."

That mattered more than I wanted it to.

I took another drink.

Somewhere deep inside me, my wolf lifted her head—alert, curious, and entirely unconcerned with caution.

Seven

Ciaran

The amber had already done its work.

Rowan sat looser in her chair now, posture less guarded, her voice warmer when she spoke. Two glasses had been more than I should have allowed, but I had weighed the risk and chosen it anyway.

I would not make that mistake again.

She watched me as I crossed to the sideboard, eyes sharp despite the haze settling in her movements.

"That's not the same," she said, nodding toward the bottle I had reached for.

"No," I replied, stopping myself before I poured. The liquid in the glass decanter was deep violet, almost luminous in the firelight. "It isn't."

"What is it?" she asked.

I turned to face her. "Something stronger than alcohol. It lowers barriers that should remain intact. For you, especially."

Her mouth curved. "You keep telling me what I *shouldn't* have."

"I am telling you because I mean it," I said. "You've already had enough."

She stood.

The movement was sudden enough that I tensed without thinking. She crossed the room with unsteady purpose, reached past me, and wrapped her fingers around the neck of the bottle.

"No," I said, more firmly this time.

She met my gaze, stubbornness flashing bright and familiar. "You said I could choose."

I should have taken it from her.

Instead, I hesitated.

She tipped the bottle back and drank—far more than a sip. A reckless swallow that stole my breath as surely as it did hers.

"Rowan—"

She lowered the bottle, laughter bubbling out of her, unrestrained and bright. "Oh. That *is* different."

I took the bottle from her before she could lift it again and set it firmly out of reach.

"That was a mistake," I said quietly.

"Maybe," she agreed, swaying slightly. "But I'm tired of being careful."

The purple liquid worked fast.

Her gaze softened, sharpened, then softened again, emotions slipping past the defenses she normally held so tight.

"I keep waiting for someone to tell me who I'm allowed to be," she said suddenly. "Ash Valley did. My pack did. Even when they said I belonged, it always came with conditions."

She looked at me, eyes too bright. Too open.

"I don't know how to exist without that," she admitted. "Without someone watching to see if I'm doing it right."

My chest tightened.

"That's why I don't want the tea," she continued, words tumbling now. "Or the rules. Or the careful choices. I just want—" She stopped, frowning as if the thought had slipped away from her. "I just want to breathe."

That was enough.

I crossed the room and steadied her with a light hand at her elbow—nothing more.

"It's time," I said. "You need rest."

She blinked up at me. "You're not sending me away."

"No," I said. "I'm walking you to your rooms."

She opened her mouth to argue, then seemed to think better of it. "All right," she said. "But only because the floor is moving."

It wasn't.

But she leaned into my space as we walked, her steps uneven, her presence a constant pressure I did not trust myself to ignore for much longer.

The corridor outside her chambers was dim and quiet, the world narrowed to stone and torchlight and the sound of her breathing beside me.

I stopped at her door.

"This is where I leave you," I said.

She turned toward me slowly, eyes dark and searching. For a moment, I thought she would thank me. Or ask a question. Or say something she would regret.

Instead, she rose onto her toes and pulled me down.

The kiss was deep. Unplanned. Unfiltered.

Her hands fisted in my coat as if anchoring herself, her mouth warm and insistent against mine. The taste of the purple liquid lingered on her lips—dangerous, intoxicating.

Shock froze me for half a heartbeat.

Then instinct roared.

I broke the kiss immediately, stepping back, control slamming into place like a locked door.

"Rowan," I said, voice rough. "Not like this."

Her eyes widened, clarity flickering in and out. "I—"

"You didn't do anything wrong," I said firmly. "But this isn't the moment."

She nodded slowly, swallowing. "Okay."

I opened the door for her, waited until she stepped inside, and did not follow.

As the door closed between us, the bond thrummed—alert, patient, entirely unsatisfied.

So was I.

Eight

Rowan

He left me at the door.

The latch clicked softly as it closed behind him, the sound far too final for how unfinished everything felt. I stood there a moment longer than necessary, hand still resting against the wood where his presence had been only seconds before.

The air felt wrong without him.

Too quiet. Too still.

My pulse refused to settle, echoing in my ears as if my body hadn't yet caught up to what had just happened. The kiss replayed itself without mercy—unexpected, deep, cut short before I could decide what I wanted it to be.

Restrained.

I exhaled slowly and forced myself to turn away from the door.

The room was warm, lamplight softening the stone walls and dulling the edges of the space. A nightgown lay folded on the bed. I changed mechanically, movements practiced, as if routine might anchor me.

It didn't.

Sleep refused to come.

I lay on my back staring at the ceiling while moonlight slipped through the narrow window, tracing pale lines across the stone. My lips still felt warm, sensitive in a way that made my chest tighten.

My wolf stirred, restless but contained.

He stopped, she observed.

"Yes," I whispered.

That mattered.

It did. More than the kiss itself.

If he had wanted to, he could have taken more. He hadn't. He had chosen control even when I hadn't given him time to prepare for what I'd done.

The thought unsettled me.

The purple liquid still hummed faintly in my veins, loosening the edges of sensation without dulling them. Everything felt closer. Sharper. My own body unfamiliar in a way that made me restless beneath the covers.

I shifted, trying to find a position that didn't make me acutely aware of myself.

It didn't help.

Tentatively, almost experimentally, I let my hand drift downward, testing pressure the way someone might test water before stepping in. The sensation startled me—heat flaring quick and bright, breath catching before I could stop it.

This was mine.

Unpracticed. Unrefined. Clumsy in its urgency.

It wasn't enough.

The realization landed quietly but firmly.

What I felt now was need without direction, sensation without anchor. There was no steadiness to it. No answering presence. Just heat that sharpened and then stalled, leaving me more aware of what was missing than what I'd found.

I stilled, hand retreating as awareness replaced impulse.

This wasn't what the kiss had promised.

I rolled onto my side and pulled the blankets closer, grounding myself in their weight. Ash Valley had taught endurance, not indulgence. Tonight, endurance was all I trusted myself with.

Eventually exhaustion dragged me under, though sleep came in fragments—

restless, shallow, unsatisfying.

I woke before dawn.

The castle was quiet—but not still.

Something held the air taut, a subtle pressure that made my wolf lift her head, alert and focused. Not danger. Not threat.

Restraint.

The realization settled slowly, bringing with it an unexpected warmth.

Ciaran was awake.

I couldn't see him, couldn't hear him, but I felt him somewhere beyond the walls—power drawn tight and held there with deliberate care, as if the control he'd shown at my door hadn't ended when he walked away.

The kiss hadn't been nothing to him.

That knowledge curled deep in my chest, unsettling and steady all at once.

As the first light of morning crept into the room, one truth became impossible to ignore.

Whatever choice I made next—staying or leaving—nothing between us would ever return to what it had been before that door closed.

And part of me didn't want it to.

Nine

Ciaran

I did not look back after leaving her door.

If I had, restraint would have failed me.

The corridor felt colder with every step I put between us, stone and shadow closing in as I forced my pace to remain measured. Control had always been my strength. Tonight, it felt stretched thin by proximity alone.

I entered my chambers and shut the door, the sound final and necessary.

Moonlight spilled across the floor in pale bands as I crossed into the bathing chamber, shedding my clothes without hesitation. The water was cold when I stepped beneath it, sharp enough to steal breath.

It did nothing.

Her scent clung to me—wolf and warmth and something deeper that resonated beneath my skin. I braced my hands against the stone wall, jaw clenched as my body refused to settle.

This was not hunger.

This was want sharpened by the bond itself.

The kiss replayed in relentless detail. The hesitation. The way she had leaned in without warning. The instant the bond surged awake—not sealed, not whole, but no longer dormant.

I had stopped because I had to.

Not because I wanted to.

Frustration simmered beneath my skin, unrelieved and unyielding. I had denied myself for centuries. Discipline had been absolute. Desire had never ruled me.

Until her.

She challenged everything. My authority. My restraint. My silence. And gods help me, it made me want to push her in return—not to take, but to see how she would stand when pressed. How she would choose when the truth was no longer distant.

Then the bond shifted.

Not sharply. Not violently.

Awareness threaded through me with deliberate precision, a ripple of sensation that was not my own. Warmth. Restlessness. A low, unsettled heat that did not belong to me yet settled unmistakably in my chest.

Rowan.

The sensation carried no image, no clarity—only need without direction, want without anchor.

She was awake.

And she was unsettled.

I swore softly, fingers tightening against the stone as the realization landed. The bond was awake enough to translate emotion now, even unsealed.

She did not know.

Not yet.

Her awareness had not opened to it. She would not feel this from me until the bond was complete, until blood and choice aligned and the connection fully awakened.

I felt her.

She felt nothing.

The imbalance cut sharper than hunger ever could.

Not ownership.

Not entitlement.

Protection.

This was dangerous.

If she pushed me, if she challenged the restraint I was holding together by will alone, the bond would respond whether I allowed it to or not. Sensation would bleed through containment. Control would become negotiation.

I shut off the water abruptly, breath uneven as I forced the bond back into silence.

This was not the time.

Not the way.

She deserved more than instinct and imbalance.

When the bond was sealed, it would be equal.

She would feel my restraint the way I felt her restlessness. The heat held deliberately in check. The want carried without release.

Until then, I would bear this alone.

I dressed quickly and crossed to the window, grounding myself in cold air and distance. If she stayed, this would become harder. If she left, the bond would not simply disappear.

Either way, this was no longer coincidence.

The bond was awake.

A soft sound behind me broke the silence.

Maeve did not knock.

She never did when she already knew the answer.

"You kissed her," she said calmly.

I did not turn. "You should not make statements you cannot prove."

She moved closer, steps unhurried. "You gave her a drink you warned her against. You sent her to bed restless and unsettled." She paused. "You kissed her."

Silence stretched.

"Yes," I said at last.

Maeve exhaled softly. "And?"

"And nothing," I replied. "I stopped."

"That is not what I asked."

I turned then, meeting her gaze.

"The bond stirred," I said carefully. "It did not seal."

Maeve's brow lifted. "Of course it didn't. You are not reckless."

"No," I agreed. "I am not."

She studied me. "You are also not untouched by this."

"How long?" she asked.

"Days," I admitted. "At first it was distant. Unformed. Tonight removed the doubt."

"And she?"

"She feels the pull," I said. "She mistakes it for attraction."

Maeve smiled faintly. "That is usually how it begins."

"It cannot continue like this," I said quietly. "She is young. Untethered. If I press too soon, she will run."

"She might run anyway," Maeve countered. "She is a wolf who has lost her pack. Control does not comfort her. Choice does."

"That is why I have given her space."

Maeve stepped closer. "You gave her space. You also gave her safety. Attention. Warmth." Her gaze sharpened. "Do not pretend you are not already courting the bond."

"That is not my intention."

"No," she said. "But it may be the outcome regardless."

I turned back to the window. "If she learns what she is to me before she chooses to stay, it will taint the choice."

"And if she stays without knowing," Maeve replied, "you risk betraying her trust."

The truth of that settled heavily.

"The Ancestors have not intervened," Maeve continued. "That alone tells me this is meant to unfold slowly."

"Slowly does not mean safely."

"No," she agreed. "It means inevitably."

The bond pulsed once in quiet agreement.

"She challenges you," Maeve said. "You like that."

"Yes," I admitted.

"And she will challenge you again."

"She already has."

Maeve softened. "You are not losing control, Ciaran. You are learning what it will cost to keep it."

She paused at the door. "Do not wait too long. Wolves feel betrayal more keenly than hunger."

"I know."

"And for what it's worth," she added, "she feels it too. More than she realizes."

The door closed behind her.

I remained at the window, the night pressing in around me, the bond awake and watchful.

Rowan did not yet know what bound us.

But she would.

And when she did, I would let her choose me with clear eyes.

Even if it broke me to wait.

Ten

Rowan

The pull did not fade with daylight.

If anything, it sharpened.

It coiled low in my chest as I dressed, followed me down the corridor, tightened with every step toward the main hall. By the time I reached the threshold, it felt alive—alert, insistent, relentless. Heat gathered between my thighs, slick and aching, my body reacting without permission.

I pressed my legs together as I walked. It didn't help.

Ciaran stood at the long table with Maeve, deep in quiet conversation.

He looked immaculate. Controlled. Composed in a way that felt deliberate—like armor worn too carefully. As if last night had been sealed away behind discipline and silence.

The lie of it settled into my bones immediately.

His head lifted the instant I entered.

The pull surged.

His gaze locked onto mine—then slid away just as quickly.

Distance.

Intentional.

My body didn't care.

Heat flared sharp and wet, my core clenching as I imagined those hands that hadn't touched me, that mouth that had stopped. I dragged in a breath through my teeth and crossed the room anyway, taking the chair directly across from him.

Maeve noticed.

She always did.

"Well," she said mildly, pouring tea. "That answers that."

"Answers what," I asked.

"That neither of you slept," she replied. "And that pretending otherwise will be pointless."

Ciaran's jaw tightened. "Maeve."

She ignored him.

"If you're done posturing," she continued, "we could all acknowledge the tension currently choking the air."

"I am not posturing," Ciaran said coolly.

I leaned forward. "Then stop backing away."

His eyes snapped to mine.

There it was. That flicker of restraint drawn too tight.

"You feel it," I said. "Whatever this is. So don't sit there and pretend you don't."

Maeve set her cup down. "Rowan."

"No," I said. "I am done being the last to know."

Ciaran folded his hands on the table—formal, contained, infuriating. "You are not ignorant."

"No," I agreed. "But you are withholding."

The pull flared again, heat spreading fast, my body betraying me as his voice wrapped low and steady around my name.

"Rowan."

It sent a shiver straight through me.

I shifted in my seat, thighs pressing together, refusing to look away. "You don't get to say my name like that and then shut me out."

Maeve exhaled. "This is escalating."

"Good," I said. "Because I want answers."

Ciaran pushed his chair back slightly—creating space.

I stood immediately, closing it.

His breath changed. Just barely.

That was all the confirmation I needed.

"You're pulling away," I said quietly. "Why."

"Because you are not steady," he replied. "And neither am I."

"Then talk to me," I said. "Touch me. Do something other than stand there pretending you're unaffected."

Maeve stood abruptly. "Absolutely not."

We both looked at her.

"You are not losing control over breakfast," she said flatly. "I refuse to explain that to the court."

"I am not losing control," Ciaran said.

"I am asking questions," I said at the same time.

Maeve pointed between us. "You are circling each other like predators who have forgotten where they are."

She turned to Ciaran. "Tell her enough to stop this before she pushes you into something neither of you can undo."

I crossed my arms. "Tell me."

Maeve's expression sobered. "This is not a werewolf bond."

The words hit harder than I expected.

"In my world," I said slowly, "bonds are chosen by the Moon Goddess. One wolf. One mate. Final."

Ciaran met my gaze. "That is not how ours work."

Maeve continued, measured. "Vampire bonds are rare. Voluntary. And when they form outside our kind…" She paused. "They change everything."

Ash Valley's threat rose sharp and immediate.

Belonging is treason.

I looked at Ciaran. "Is that why you won't explain it?"

"Yes," he said without hesitation.

Maeve straightened. "I'm leaving before you tear each other apart."

She paused beside me. "This isn't a trap, Rowan."

Then she was gone.

The room felt tighter without her.

I faced Ciaran. "Now talk."

He stood—slow, grounded, careful not to crowd me.

"You were born into assigned bonds," he said. "We are not."

"So you choose," I said.

"Yes."

"And this?" I gestured between us.

"This is recognition."

The word sent a chill through me.

"And if I refuse?"

"It remains dormant."

"And if I accept?"

"It becomes equal."

Heat surged again, sharper now, focused.

"Then prove it," I said.

His eyes darkened. "How."

"Kiss me," I said. "And stop pretending this is nothing."

He stepped closer—then stopped himself, restraint vibrating through the space between us.

"Be careful," he said quietly. "Because once I answer that, there is no distance left to hide behind."

I lifted my chin. "Then stop hiding."

The bond surged.

This time, he didn't step away.

And neither did I.

Eleven

Rowan

The silence between us was alive.

It pressed against my skin, thick and charged, the pull humming so loudly in my chest it drowned out thought. I felt him before he touched me—felt the restraint coiled tight beneath his stillness, the way he held himself back as if holding the world together by force alone.

"You are certain," Ciaran said quietly.

My pulse was everywhere. "I'm done being afraid of what I feel."

His gaze dropped to my throat.

The pull surged—hot, aching, demanding—as if my body answered before my mind could catch up.

He crossed the distance in two measured steps and stopped just short of touching me. The heat from him was overwhelming, close enough that if I leaned forward my breasts would brush his chest. My breath quickened, my body betraying me with want that had nowhere to go.

"This is not how it ends," he said, voice rough now. "Once this begins, it does not fade."

"I know," I whispered. "I still want it."

Something in him gave—not control, but composure.

His hand lifted, fingers brushing my jaw with reverent restraint. The touch alone sent heat spiraling through me, my body leaning into him before I could stop myself.

Then his mouth was on mine.

The kiss burned.

Slow and deep, controlled in a way that made my knees weaken. His lips moved with intent, drawing a sound from my throat that felt stolen and entirely my own. I pressed closer, hands clutching at his coat, desperate for more.

He broke the kiss abruptly, breath ragged.

"Rowan," he said. "You don't understand what you're offering."

"I understand enough," I said, shaking. "I trust you."

The pull flared bright and unbearable.

Without thinking, I tilted my head back, exposing my throat.

Offering.

"Please."

His entire body went still.

For a heartbeat I thought he would refuse.

Then his hand slid to my waist, firm and grounding, holding me exactly where I was as his mouth lowered—not to bite, not yet—but to my skin. His lips traced slowly along my throat, sending sparks racing down my spine.

I gasped.

"Stay still," he murmured. "Let me guide this."

His other hand moved lower, deliberate and unhurried, sliding between my thighs. The contact shattered me. I cried out, hips jerking instinctively, my body already slick and aching.

"Ciaran—"

"I know," he said, voice strained. "I feel it."

His fingers worked me with devastating precision, not hurried, not rough—controlled in a way that made the sensation unbearable. My body arched into his touch, pleasure climbing fast and sharp, stealing thought and breath.

Right as the pressure crested, his mouth returned to my throat.

His fangs pierced my skin.

The world broke open.

Pleasure detonated through me in a white-hot rush, deeper and more consuming than anything I had ever known. My cry tore free as my body shattered around his fingers, sensation flooding through me as the bond flared fully awake.

Heat. Power. Connection.

Too much.

He held me through it, arms locking around me as my release tore through me, his control the only thing keeping me upright as the bond surged—raw, blazing, incomplete but undeniable.

Then he stopped.

Pulled back.

His fangs withdrew, his mouth sealing the bite as if to steady us both. His breath was ragged, his eyes glowing faintly as he pressed his forehead to mine.

"That's enough," he said hoarsely. "If I go further, I won't stop."

I trembled in his arms, the bond still roaring through me, my body sensitive and wrecked.

"Ciaran," I breathed.

He cupped my face gently. Reverently. "The bond is open," he said. "But it is not finished. And neither are you."

I swallowed hard. "You're stopping."

"Yes."

It hurt more than I expected.

"I won't take you while you're burning," he continued. "That belongs to later. When you're steady. When the choice is clear."

He set me back on my feet slowly, hands lingering just long enough to remind me this was real. That *he* was real.

The bond pulsed between us—alive, open, unresolved.

The room felt too small. Too charged.

"I need to leave," I said suddenly, panic and longing colliding hard in my chest.

He didn't stop me.

That restraint cut deeper than anything else.

I turned and ran.

The corridors blurred as I fled, heart racing, the bond pulling painfully with every step. My skin still sang where his mouth had been, my body humming with sensation I didn't know how to carry yet.

I barely registered where I was going.

Until the scent hit me.

Ciaran.

I froze inside his room, panic flaring sharp and immediate. I turned for the door—then stopped as the bond surged again, fierce and anchoring.

Not claiming.

Holding.

My legs gave out.

I sank onto the edge of his bed, fingers curling into the sheets as exhaustion crashed over me. His scent wrapped around me, deep and overwhelming, and despite myself, my breathing slowed.

This wasn't safety.

It was proximity.

And I didn't yet know the difference.

My eyes slid closed before I could stop them.

The bond remained—open.

Unfinished.

Waiting.

Twelve

Ciaran

I felt her before I saw her.

The bond pulled sharp and immediate the moment I stepped into my chambers, awareness striking so hard it rooted me in place. The room was dark, the air heavy with familiarity and something newly unsettled.

Her scent.

Wolf. Heat. Rowan.

My gaze went to the bed.

She lay curled on her side, hair fanned across the pillow, breathing slow and uneven. For a long moment, I could only stand there, the reality of her presence landing deeper than any blow.

She had run.

And somehow, she had come here.

The bond surged in response—not contentment, not peace, but a restless pull that tightened my chest. It reacted to proximity the way it always would now: awake, demanding, unfinished.

She stirred, brows drawing together as if sensing me.

"Ciaran," she whispered, pushing up on one elbow. "I didn't mean to—"

"You're safe," I said immediately, crossing the room in two strides.

She swayed, exhaustion overtaking adrenaline. I caught her easily before she could fall, lifting her into my arms with care. Her body fit against mine too easily, the bond flaring hard at the contact.

I carried her fully onto the bed and settled her against the pillows, pulling the covers up around her. My hands lingered only long enough to ensure she was warm and steady.

She looked at me, eyes glassy with lingering fear and something softer beneath it.

"I shouldn't be here," she murmured.

"You shouldn't be alone," I corrected quietly.

Her eyelids fluttered, the weight of the bond and exhaustion dragging her under before she could argue.

I remained seated at her side.

The mark at her throat had already begun to fade, but the memory of her taste lingered—bright and dangerous. Stopping had cost me more than I wanted to admit.

I wanted her.

Not just her body—though the pull was relentless—but her presence. Her refusal to be small. The way she filled space without apology.

That was what frightened me.

I removed my boots quietly and lay back against the far edge of the bed, careful not to touch her again. Even distance was effort now.

Sleep took me without warning.

—

We stood in a place that was not a place.

Light and shadow wove together, neither dominant nor absent. Rowan stood across from me, whole and bright, her wolf visible now—no longer restrained, but alert and wary.

"You feel it now," the Ancestors said. Many voices. One will.

The bond stretched between us, visible as threads of light—uneven, taut, unfinished.

"This bond was not assigned," they continued. "It was recognized."

Images unfolded.

Two paths.

One sealed by blood freely given and returned—power balanced, sensation shared, strength unlocked fully.

The other left open—aching, draining, never quite fading.

"To unlock it," the voices said, "both must choose with clarity. Blood must be exchanged in balance. Desire must be matched by intent."

Rowan turned to me, eyes steady.

"What happens if we accept it?"

Strength—but cost. Her wolf awakened fully. My power unbound from ancestral restraint.

"And if we refuse?"

"The bond waits," they said. "And it takes."

The truth landed hard.

Then the space dimmed, leaving only me.

"You hesitate."

"I fear taking from her."

"She is not fragile," the Ancestors replied. "But she is becoming."

"And if she leaves?"

"Then you will endure," they said. "But you will not be unchanged."

I woke with a sharp breath.

Dawn light spilled across the room.

Rowan slept nearby, her presence pulling at the bond like an open wound. It throbbed now—active, unresolved, draining.

I rose quietly, crossing to the window, grounding myself in cold air.

The bond did not quiet.

It demanded.

She shifted in her sleep, drawn by instinct, not comfort.

I did not pull her closer.

I would not take more.

I would wait.

For her certainty.

For her choice.

Until then, restraint would cost me everything.

And I would pay it. At least that's what I kept telling my self, as I slowly climbed back into my bed.

Thirteen

Rowan

I woke wrapped in heat.

Not the frantic, spiraling heat from the night before—but something deeper. Heavier. Like my body had remembered something my mind was still catching up to.

Ciaran lay behind me, solid and unmistakable, his chest rising slowly against my back. His arm was draped over my waist, loose but deliberate, as if he had pulled me close sometime during the night and never let go.

One hand rested on my hip.

The other—

I froze.

His palm was cupped fully over my breast, fingers curved as though they belonged there. Warm. Heavy. Possessive in a way that sent a sharp pulse straight between my thighs.

He was still asleep.

I could hear it in his breathing—slow, even, controlled. No tension. No restraint pulled tight.

My heart began to race anyway.

Carefully, I shifted, testing the space between us.

That was when I felt it.

Hard.

Pressed unmistakably against the curve of my ass.

"Oh," I whispered.

My wolf stirred immediately, alert and curious rather than alarmed.

That is not fear, she observed.

"No," I agreed silently, heat blooming low and insistent. "It's… not."

The bond hummed in response, alive and watchful. Not demanding. Just aware.

Fragments of the night before surfaced—his mouth at my throat, the bite, the way pleasure had shattered through me so violently I had nearly lost myself to it. The way he had stopped. The way he had held me instead of taking more.

My body remembered everything.

And wanted more.

I shifted again, slower this time, letting my hip roll just enough that I brushed against him. His breath changed instantly—deepening, catching.

He woke.

Not with a start. Not with confusion.

With awareness.

"Rowan," he murmured against my neck.

The sound of my name on his lips sent a sharp, aching pulse straight to my core. I sucked in a breath, heat curling tighter, slickness gathering without permission.

"You're awake," I said, my voice rougher than I intended.

"Yes," he replied quietly. "You moved."

I turned carefully in his arms until I could see his face. His eyes were open now—dark, intent, already too aware of everything between us. His gaze dropped immediately to my mouth.

"The bond," I whispered. "It's louder."

He nodded once. "It will be. After blood."

My pulse jumped.

"And you?" I asked softly. "You feel it too."

"Yes."

The admission landed like a spark in dry tinder.

I leaned in without thinking. He met me halfway.

The kiss was slow at first—testing, deliberate—but the moment our mouths met, the bond flared hot and bright, sensation snapping sharp and immediate. His lips parted against mine, controlled but hungry, and I moaned softly as heat spilled through me.

His hand tightened on my hip.

Then—just as suddenly—he pulled back.

"No," he said, breath uneven. "We should slow."

The words felt like cold water.

I stared at him. "Why."

His jaw tightened. "Because you are new to this. Because last night awakened things you don't yet understand. Because I will not take your first time while your body is burning and your bond is shouting over your consent."

Anger flared sharp and bright.

"I am not fragile," I snapped.

"I know," he said immediately. "That is exactly why this matters."

I pushed myself up, straddling his hips before he could stop me. His breath hitched sharply as my heat brushed against him through the thin barrier of fabric.

"You are not taking anything," I said fiercely. "I am choosing."

"Rowan—"

I cut him off by kissing him again, harder this time. Open-mouthed. Demanding. I ground down against him deliberately, feeling just how affected he already was, and the knowledge sent a thrill through me.

His hands came up instinctively—to steady me, to stop me—but I felt the hesitation there. The restraint.

It infuriated me.

I broke the kiss and leaned back just far enough to look at him.

"You feel this too," I said. "Don't pretend you don't."

"I do," he said hoarsely. "That's the problem."

"No," I said. "That's the truth."

Before he could respond, I leaned forward and bit him.

Not gently.

My teeth sank into the skin of his shoulder, sharp and deliberate. I tasted him instantly—iron and heat and something unmistakably *alive*. His blood flooded my mouth, and the bond screamed in response, power surging so hard it stole my breath.

Ciaran swore violently, his body jerking beneath me.

"Rowan—"

I pulled back, startled at my own boldness, and realized my lip stung sharply.

I had bitten myself too.

Blood welled there, metallic and warm.

He froze.

Completely still.

His gaze snapped to my mouth, pupils blown wide, breath shallow and broken. The scent of blood filled the air—mine and his—and the bond roared awake, no longer patient.

"You are bleeding," he said, voice wrecked.

"I don't care," I said, dragging my thumb across my lip and smearing it deliberately. "I want you."

That broke him.

A sound tore from his chest—low, raw, unrestrained—as he surged upright, hands gripping my hips hard enough to bruise. He crushed his mouth to mine, tasting blood and heat and need all at once, and the kiss turned feral instantly.

Clothes became obstacles.

His hands tore my nightgown apart, fabric ripping open as he dragged it off my body. Cool air hit my bare skin, but his mouth and hands were everywhere—my breasts, my throat, my stomach—marking, claiming, worshiping in equal measure.

I gasped as his mouth closed around my nipple, sucking hard enough to make my back arch, pleasure spiking sharp and blinding. My fingers fisted in his hair, holding him there as he groaned against me.

"Still want this?" he demanded, voice rough and dark.

"Yes," I sobbed. "Please."

He surged back up, lifting me effortlessly and laying me back against the bed. His mouth trailed fire down my body, teeth grazing, tongue soothing, until he settled between my thighs.

When his mouth touched me there, I cried out.

The bond turned it into something overwhelming—every flick of his tongue echoed through me, magnified and relentless. My hips bucked instinctively, fingers digging into the sheets as pleasure coiled tight and snapped again and again.

I shattered under his mouth, coming hard enough that I screamed his name.

He didn't stop.

Only when I was trembling and boneless did he rise again, eyes glowing faintly, control hanging by a thread.

"This is your choice," he said one last time. "Say it."

"I choose you," I said without hesitation.

That was enough.

He pressed into me slowly, deliberately, giving me time to breathe through the stretch, through the unfamiliar intensity. It burned briefly—sharp and overwhelming—but the pleasure followed fast, deep and consuming.

I wrapped my legs around him, pulling him closer, urging him on.

The bond sang.

Every movement was amplified—his pleasure spilling into mine, my reactions feeding back into him. We moved together, clumsy and desperate and perfect, until sensation overtook thought entirely.

When I came again, it tore through me, bright and blinding.

He followed with a groan that vibrated through my bones, burying himself deep as the bond flared hot and wild between us.

For a moment, there was nothing but breath and heat and the echo of power still settling through my body.

Then exhaustion crashed over me all at once.

My eyes fluttered.

"Ciaran," I murmured.

"I'm here," he said immediately, gathering me close, careful again, controlled once more now that the moment had passed.

Sleep claimed me before I could say anything else.

The bond pulsed once—slow, deep.

Unsealed.

Waiting.

Fourteen

Rowan

I woke with the bond singing softly under my skin.

Not loud like it had been when it first snapped awake—bright and blinding and too big for my body to hold—but steady now. Present. Like a second heartbeat that had learned my rhythm, close and constant without fully claiming me.

Ciaran was still asleep beside me.

That alone felt impossible.

His arm was heavy around my waist, his chest warm against my back, breath even at my neck. The castle was quiet in the way only stone could be quiet—thick walls holding the world at a distance. Somewhere beyond them, dawn was happening. In here, everything was still.

I shifted slightly, testing the reality of it.

The bond responded immediately, a slow pulse that hummed through my bones—not demanding, not possessive, simply aware. My wolf lifted her head inside me, not restless now, not trapped behind the familiar wall, but alert and…content.

We did it, she said simply.

My throat tightened. Yes.

And still, the strangest part wasn't the bite marks on my skin or the lingering ache in my body. It wasn't the way my mind kept replaying the night like it was trying to convince itself it had happened.

The strangest part was the absence of loneliness.

I had lived with it for so long I hadn't realized it was a constant until it was gone.

I turned carefully, rolling onto my side to face him.

Ciaran looked younger asleep—less carved from control, less weighed down by centuries of choosing restraint. His lashes rested dark against his cheekbones, mouth relaxed, hair fallen across the pillow in uneven strands. If he had been human, he would have looked almost peaceful.

But he wasn't human.

And neither, it seemed, was my life anymore.

I reached up, hovering my fingers near the faded mark at his throat. I didn't touch. Not yet.

Not because I was afraid of him.

Because I was afraid of how quickly wanting him had become familiar.

My wolf made a low sound that felt like approval.

Stop thinking like you're still alone, she murmured.

I swallowed hard. I don't know how to be anything else.

She pressed closer, warm and steady. Then we learn.

The bed shifted.

Ciaran's eyes opened without warning, dark and clear like he'd never truly been asleep at all. His gaze found mine instantly, and the bond tightened—gentle, not demanding, but present in a way that made my breath catch.

For a heartbeat, neither of us spoke.

Then he exhaled, slow and controlled, and I felt it through the bond—relief threaded with reverence.

"You're awake," he murmured.

"Yes." My voice sounded rough. I cleared my throat. "So are you."

His mouth curved faintly. "I was awake the moment you thought my name."

Heat moved low in my body at the implication, and my wolf purred like she was pleased with herself.

I did not look away. Not this time. "Is that how it is now?"

His gaze dipped briefly to my throat, then returned to my eyes. "Not always. Not like a constant intrusion. But yes…we will sense each other."

"That sounds dangerous."

"It can be," he said quietly. "If either of us tries to use it as control."

Something in his tone made my spine straighten. Not warning—promise.

I nodded once, accepting it.

The bond pulsed in agreement.

He shifted closer, careful, as if he was still measuring the edge of what I could take. His fingers brushed my cheek—gentle, grounding—before his hand slid to the back of my neck, thumb resting there like an anchor.

"I don't know what happens now," I admitted.

"Now you breathe," Ciaran said. "You eat. You recover."

"And after that?"

"After that," he said, voice low, "we learn each other."

"That sounds like a polite way to avoid questions."

A faint smile. "It is a polite way to avoid overwhelming you."

"I'm already overwhelmed," I said quietly. "But I'd rather be overwhelmed by truth than kept safe with ignorance."

He was still for a long moment, weighing.

"Then ask."

My throat tightened.

"Do you know anything about Ash Valley?"

The bond reacted—subtle tension, awareness sharpening.

"I know of them," he said. "Not intimately."

"My parents died when I was little," I said. "It was an accident. That's what they told me."

He didn't interrupt. Didn't look away.

"I don't remember them well. Just pieces. The smell of my mother's hair. My father's hands. Big. Calloused. Safe."

"They said a border patrol went wrong. Rogues crossed at night. My parents died protecting the line." I swallowed. "But no one ever let me ask questions."

"What do you suspect?" he asked softly.

"I don't know. That's the problem."

"You deserved the truth," he said.

My breath hitched.

"And you deserve it still."

"I was an orphan before exile," I whispered. "But exile made it public."

"They made you a scapegoat."

"Yes."

"And they warned you to remain unaligned."

My jaw tightened. "If I belong anywhere else, they call it treason."

"And answer it with death."

"I'm not afraid of dying."

"I believe you."

"I'm afraid," I admitted, "that I'll start wanting something and not know how to stop."

"Then we don't rush," he said.

"I want to learn. Not just react."

"Then we will."

A pause.

"Stay," I whispered.

"I am here," he said. "I'm not going anywhere."

The bond pulsed, certain.

I shifted closer, forehead to his. The touch was gentle, intimate.

Then my body remembered.

Heat curled low and sharp, familiar now. Want rising fast, fed by memory and choice instead of confusion.

Ciaran exhaled against my mouth, voice rough. "Tell me what you want."

"I want—"

His mouth crashed onto mine, devouring, tongue thrusting deep as if claiming every inch. I tangled my fingers in his hair, holding him there while my legs parted instinctively. Ciaran's hand trailed down my stomach, slipping under my waistband to cup my mound, fingers parting my folds to stroke through the wetness gathering there. I whimpered into the kiss, hips bucking as he circled my clit with precise pressure, building the ache until it bordered on pain.

He pulled back, eyes locked on mine, and stripped me bare with efficient tugs, his own clothes following in a heap on the floor. His cock stood rigid, veins prominent, tip glistening. I reached for it, wrapping my hand around the base and pumping slowly, watching his jaw clench with the effort to hold back. Ciaran knocked my hand away gently, then flipped me onto my stomach, lifting my hips until I was on all fours.

"Like this," he murmured, positioning himself behind me. The head of his cock nudged my entrance, teasing before he thrust in fully, burying himself to the hilt. I cried out at the sudden fullness, pussy stretching around him as he set a relentless pace, hips snapping forward. His hands gripped my waist, pulling me back onto each stroke, balls slapping against my skin. I pushed back, meeting him thrust for thrust, the angle letting him grind against that sensitive spot inside.

Sweat dripped down his chest onto my back, his grunts mixing with my moans. One hand slid up to pinch my nipple, rolling it between fingers while the other reached around to rub my clit in tight circles. The dual assault shattered me—I came hard, walls fluttering and squeezing his cock, milking him as tremors shook my body. Ciaran's rhythm faltered, then he drove deep one final time, spilling inside me with a guttural roar, hot spurts coating my depths.

He eased out slowly, gathering me into his arms as we both caught our breath.

After, I lay against him, breathing slow, heart steady, the bond quieting into warmth instead of fire.

Ciaran's fingers combed through my hair absentmindedly, the gesture so human it undid me all over again.

My wolf sighed, satisfied.

Not because of sex.

Because for the first time in my life, I had said the truth out loud.

And it had been held gently instead of used against me.

Fifteen

Rowan

The day moved differently after the bond opened.

Not settled. Not complete.

Alive in a way that refused to be ignored.

I felt Ciaran everywhere—not like possession, not like certainty, but like a current I couldn't step out of. A thread pulled too tight, humming under my skin whether I acknowledged it or not. The castle itself no longer felt like somewhere I was passing through.

It felt like somewhere I was *reacting* inside.

Maeve brought food and pretended not to notice the faint marks at my throat or the way my posture had shifted—less guarded, more volatile. She didn't ask questions. Didn't smirk. She only said, "Eat. You'll need it," and left as if she already understood what instability looked like.

Ciaran left briefly—court matters, borders, obligations he couldn't fully escape. He told me he would return.

And he did.

Exactly when he said he would.

That mattered more than it should have.

We sat near the window overlooking the forest, gray light filtering through layered clouds. The trees swayed gently, but my wolf was not calm. She paced inside me, restless and alert.

Not fear.

Anticipation.

"You feel it," Ciaran said quietly.

"I always feel the forest," I replied. "Even when I can't…be what I'm supposed to be."

His attention sharpened. "Tell me."

I swallowed. "My wolf talks to me."

He didn't interrupt.

"She always has. Not constantly. Just…presence. Instinct." I hesitated. "I can feel when I'm supposed to shift. I can feel my body approach the edge. And then it stops."

My wolf huffed.

It is not refusal, she said. *It is restraint.*

The word slipped out of me before I could stop it. "Restraint."

Ciaran's brows lifted slightly. "You speak to her aloud."

"Sometimes."

"I don't mind."

That shouldn't have mattered. It did.

Ash Valley had trained control into my bones. Strength meant suppression. Surrender meant weakness. Even shifting felt like something you earned by never letting go.

"I've never had a heat," I admitted.

Ciaran stilled.

"I assumed I never would," I continued. "Because nothing about me ever followed the rules."

"And now?" he asked.

Now my body wasn't waiting for permission.

Now sensation arrived before thought.

"I don't know what rules apply to me," I said honestly. "And I'm afraid of waking up one day and not recognizing myself."

"Then we don't let it happen *to* you," Ciaran said. "We face it together."

The bond pulsed—too fast, too bright.

That was when it started to go wrong.

Heat didn't rise naturally.

It *spiked.*

Emotion bled across the bond without filter—my fear, my need, my confusion, my want—all of it hitting him at once. I felt it rebound immediately, amplified, distorted, impossible to separate from my own body.

My wolf paced harder.

This is not balance, she warned.

Ciaran inhaled sharply.

"Rowan," he said, and I felt the strain in it. Not desire. Overload.

"I can feel you," he admitted. "And it isn't…clear."

I wasn't thinking clearly either.

The bond tightened, misaligned, feeding sensation faster than intention could keep up. Touch became grounding. Proximity became necessary.

Ciaran tried to slow it. I felt him try—felt control brace and fracture under the weight of everything I was pouring into him without meaning to.

"This is dangerous," he said once.

And then the bond surged again, unfiltered.

His restraint snapped.

This was different. Not calm. Not choice settling into certainty.

This was the bond refusing to stay quiet.

It pulsed again—too warm, too intimate—sending sensation through me before I could brace for it. My body remembered faster than my mind could follow. Heat curled low, sharper than earlier, like a spark catching where it shouldn't have. Ciaran's gaze darkened, his breath hitching as the bond carried my confusion, my want, my fear straight into him without filter.

"You feel it," he murmured, but there was strain in his voice now.

"Yes," I said, though the word felt like it arrived after the sensation, not before.

"Tell me what you want," he said softly, and I felt his control pull tight—bracing, not inviting.

"I want to stop being afraid of what I want," I answered, the truth slipping out because the bond demanded honesty.

Something in him snapped—not desire, not dominance, but restraint failing under the weight of everything bleeding across the bond. He leaned in, mouth brushing mine, slow and careful as if trying to anchor us both, as if restraint might still hold.

Then the spark flared.

His lips pressed harder, hunger overtaking caution as the bond surged again, amplifying every sensation. I gripped his shoulders, pulling him closer as the kiss deepened, teeth nipping at each other's lips. His hands roamed down my sides, fingers digging into my hips with frustrated urgency before yanking my shirt up and over my head. He broke the kiss only long enough to toss it aside, then latched onto my neck, sucking hard enough to leave marks, his palms cupping my breasts as his thumbs circled my nipples—touch driven less by intent than by the bond demanding more.

I gasped, arching into his touch, my hands fumbling with his belt more out of instinct than intention. The bond thrummed wildly between us, amplifying everything—my heat, my need, my confusion—until my skin felt electric, oversensitive, wrong in a way that demanded release. He growled low in his throat as I freed his cock, thick and hard, pulsing in my grip, and the bond flared hard enough that I felt his reaction echo back through me. I stroked him once, twice, feeling him twitch as pre-cum slicked my palm, sensation feeding sensation in a loop neither of us could slow.

Ciaran shoved my pants down roughly, not from impatience but because the bond gave him no space to think. His hand dove between my thighs, finding me already wet and aching, my body responding faster than my mind could catch up.

"Fuck, Rowan," he rasped, fingers plunging inside me, curling to hit that spot that made my knees buckle as the bond surged again. I moaned, riding his hand as he pumped in and out, his thumb grinding against my clit, pressure building too fast, too sharp—overload instead of anticipation. I didn't want to wait. I couldn't. I pushed him back onto the bed and straddled his hips, guiding his cock to my entrance because the bond demanded completion it couldn't yet achieve.

Sinking down, I took him inch by inch, the stretch burning and blinding as my body struggled to adjust, sensation crashing through me in uneven waves. We moved together without rhythm at first, desperate and uncoordinated, my hips rolling as I fucked him deep, his hands gripping my ass hard enough to bruise as if grounding himself through contact alone. Sweat slicked our skin, breaths ragged and broken, the bond screaming too loudly to ignore.

He sat up suddenly, mouth capturing a nipple, sucking and biting while thrusting up into me, the sensation tearing a sound from my throat as the bond surged—too hot, too fast, shoving us both toward something neither of us was ready for. The pull to bite slammed into me without warning. Not hunger. Not instinct alone. Recognition. Claim. Acceptance.

I leaned forward on a broken gasp, teeth scraping his shoulder, his collarbone—*not breaking skin*, but close enough that my body shook with the effort to stop. Ciaran froze for half a heartbeat, breath tearing from his chest as his own teeth pressed against my throat in answer, restrained only by the last thread of control he still possessed.

We both knew what that edge meant.

The bond howled for blood.

For sealing.

For completion.

Neither of us gave in.

The denial only intensified everything—pleasure sharpening, pressure coiling tighter, the open bond feeding sensation back on itself until I shattered around him with a cry, my body clenching hard enough to drag his own release from him moments later. He thrust deep, groaning my name like it was a confession, holding me there as the aftershocks tore through us both.

I cried out, clenching around his cock as orgasm tore through me, heat pulsing violently from my core, my wolf howling in restless approval. Ciaran followed seconds later, groaning as he slammed up one last time, spilling inside me as the bond flared hot and unbalanced, giving without settling. We collapsed together, still joined, his arms wrapping around me tight—not possessive, but bracing.

After, I lay against him, breath uneven, the bond humming quietly as if it thought it had succeeded—temporarily.

But my wolf was not content.

She paced inside me, alert and impatient, as if she could already feel the moon on the horizon, even through stone walls.

Sixteen

Ciaran

The bond changed everything.

Not in the way humans expected. There were no violent surges, no sudden loss of self. Instead, it rewired the smallest things first. Awareness sharpened. Distance became measurable. Silence gained texture.

Rowan slept for a few hours after the bond sealed, exhaustion finally overtaking what adrenaline and instinct had carried. I did not sleep.

I sat at the window in my chambers and watched the forest shift in the wind, my thoughts precise, restless. The bond thrummed beneath my ribs like a living thread, responsive to every movement she made in the adjoining room.

Not pain.

Not hunger.

Connection.

It would have been easy to mistake that connection for entitlement. To believe the bond meant possession.

It did not.

The bond was not a chain.

It was a bridge.

And bridges only held when both sides chose to stand.

I had chosen her.

Now I had to keep proving that her choice mattered.

A knock sounded.

Maeve entered without waiting. Her gaze swept me once, lingering briefly on the faint marks at my throat, on the way the bond no longer strained against restraint but sat integrated into my posture.

"Well," she said. "It's done."

"It's sealed," I corrected.

Maeve's brow lifted. "And you think that makes it less final?"

I didn't answer.

She crossed the room and poured herself a drink. "The court will notice."

"They always do."

"And Rowan?"

"She's adjusting."

Maeve's mouth curved faintly. "Or you are."

She leaned against the table. "Tell me you warned her about convergence."

Silence tightened.

"I haven't," I admitted.

Maeve's expression hardened. "Then you're gambling with her trust."

"I'm trying not to frighten her with a future she hasn't felt."

"And what will frighten her more," Maeve countered, "is waking up inside it without understanding why."

She was right. I disliked the word *convergence* because it sounded clinical. But it was accurate.

The bond between vampire and wolf was rare. Voluntary. Powerful. And it came with a period of alignment—when blood, instinct, and magic recalibrated until both bodies could hold what had been joined.

Rowan was already near the threshold.

I could feel it in the way the bond warmed when she was close. In the way her wolf paced beneath her skin. In the subtle shift of her scent—sharper, deeper, as if her body were preparing for something long denied.

Heat, in wolves, was lunar.

Convergence was something else.

It was the bond insisting the bridge be crossed fully.

And it could drown the unprepared.

"I won't let it take her," I said quietly.

Maeve softened slightly. "Then you must tell her."

I stared out at the forest. "How do I explain that her body may soon demand what her mind hasn't learned to hold?"

"By reminding her she has choice," Maeve said. "Even inside want."

She paused. "The full moon is close."

"I know."

"And she still believes she cannot shift."

That truth weighed heavily. The bond did not simply connect us—it balanced us. If Rowan's wolf had been suppressed by fear and exile, sealing the bond may have removed the final restraint.

Her first shift could come violently.

Or suddenly.

Or both.

"I'll be with her," I said.

Maeve nodded. "Good. Because if she shifts alone, she may not recognize herself."

After she left, the room felt emptier—but my awareness remained full, threaded through stone and distance, anchored to Rowan.

When I reached her door, I paused.

I listened with the bond.

She was awake. Restless. And beneath it, something coiled—warmth gathering like a storm not yet broken.

I knocked once and entered.

Seventeen

Rowan

It started as warmth.

Not arousal—not exactly—but something deeper, slower. Like heat sinking into bone instead of skin. I noticed it the moment I woke, tangled in sheets that suddenly felt too heavy, too close, my body restless in a way that had nothing to do with dreams.

My wolf stirred immediately.

This is it, she said.

My heart jumped. *This is what?*

Alignment.

The bond hummed under my skin, brighter than it had been the night before, no longer content to stay quiet. It pulsed with awareness, with insistence, like it was checking every part of me to see what fit and what resisted.

I swung my legs over the side of the bed and had to brace myself against the mattress.

The room tilted.

Not dizziness—something else. Sensation sharpened too quickly. The cool air felt too cool. The fabric of my shirt scraped in a way that made my skin prickle. Every sound carried too much weight.

My wolf paced, claws clicking faintly against the inside of my ribs.

You are not breaking, she said. *You are opening.*

"I don't like it," I muttered aloud.

She snorted. *You don't like not being in control.*

She wasn't wrong.

I dressed slowly, deliberately, grounding myself in familiar motions. Boots. Braid. Breath. By the time I stepped into the corridor, the heat had settled into something coiled instead of overwhelming—tight, watchful, waiting.

Ciaran felt it the moment he saw me.

The bond tightened—sharp, responsive—and his posture shifted subtly, control snapping into place like armor. His gaze tracked me from head to toe, lingering not possessively, but as if he were reading signs written beneath my skin.

"You feel different," he said quietly.

"So do you," I replied.

"This isn't lunar heat," I said after a moment. "Not the way wolves mean it."

"No," he agreed. "It's not lunar."

"What is it, then?"

He hesitated, just long enough that I knew the answer wouldn't be simple.

"It's the bond insisting on equilibrium," he said finally. "Your body is adjusting to carrying shared power."

"And the want?" I asked. "The way everything feels…too much?"

"That," he said, voice lower, "is because the bond doesn't distinguish between emotional alignment and physical expression."

I crossed my arms. "That sounds like a polite way to say this is going to get worse."

The corner of his mouth lifted faintly. "Yes."

My wolf huffed, pleased.

"And if I say stop?" I asked.

"Then we stop," he said immediately.

No hesitation. No qualifiers.

The bond warmed at the certainty.

I nodded once. "Then I want to understand it. Not be swept into it."

"Then stay with me today," he said. "Where I can watch the changes."

The implication wasn't confinement.

It was care.

I considered it, then nodded. "All right."

The heat coiled tighter in response, anticipation sparking through it.

I stepped closer, the narrow hallway pressing in around us like the bond itself—unyielding, intimate. Ciaran's scent wrapped around me, woodsmoke and earth, sharpening the ache low in my belly. My wolf urged me forward, not with frenzy, but with a steady pull, like gravity aligning two stars.

I reached out, fingers brushing his chest, feeling the rapid thump of his heart through his shirt. The bond lit up, sending a jolt straight to my core, my body clenching with sudden need. Ciaran's eyes locked on mine, pupils dilating—but he held still, waiting.

"Show me," I whispered, my voice rougher than intended. "What it feels like when we...balance."

His hand caught my wrist, thumb stroking my pulse. The touch rippled through me—warmth blooming in my veins, tightening everything beneath my skin. He pulled me flush against him, the hard line of him pressing into my hip through our clothes. I gasped, the bond humming approval, every nerve alight.

Ciaran's other hand slid to my lower back, dipping just under my waistband to grip the curve of my ass. He squeezed—firm, grounding—drawing a sound from my throat before I could stop it.

"Tell me to stop," he murmured against my ear, breath hot. "And I will."

But I didn't want to stop.

I tilted my head and captured his mouth in a kiss that started slow and ignited fast—tongues tangling, teeth grazing as hunger surged between us. My hands roamed, yanking his shirt free, nails scraping over taut muscle. The bond amplified everything, his pleasure echoing in my skin until my body throbbed with it.

He spun us, backing me against the cool stone wall, the contrast sending shivers down my spine. One knee nudged my legs apart as his hand slid between my thighs, pressure building through fabric in slow, deliberate circles.

"More," I demanded, fumbling with his belt.

He helped, movements efficient and strained, control fraying at the edges. The bond wove tighter with every touch, sensation doubling, blurring where I ended and he began.

When release came, it came hard and sudden—my body locking, my breath breaking as the bond surged bright and overwhelming. I bit down on his shoulder to keep from crying out, the shared peak sending him shuddering with me.

After, he held me there until my knees steadied, easing us back into order with careful hands, though his touch lingered, tracing the heat still burning beneath my skin.

I leaned into him, breaths syncing, the ache in my bones quieter—but not gone.

This was only the beginning.

Eighteen

Rowan

By midday, there was no mistaking it.

The warmth had sharpened into an edge—threaded through my nerves, settling low in my body, demanding attention. It came in waves, stealing breath and loosening knees, then retreating just enough to make me doubt myself.

My wolf paced constantly now, pressing against my skin like she wanted out.

Soon, she said again. Stronger this time.

I paced the length of the sitting room, bare feet whispering over stone. The windows were open, forest air spilling in, but it wasn't enough. Everything felt close. Too close.

Ciaran watched me from across the room, posture deliberately relaxed, hands clasped behind his back like he was holding himself together by will alone.

The bond between us thrummed—hot, bright, alive.

"You're doing that on purpose," I accused, stopping abruptly.

His brow lifted. "Doing what."

"Staying away," I said. "You're holding yourself back so hard I can feel it."

His jaw tightened. "Yes."

"Why?"

"Because if I don't," he said carefully, "the bond will pull us into expression instead of awareness."

I laughed softly, breathless. "You say that like it's a bad thing."

"For now," he said, eyes darkening, "it could be."

The heat surged at the look alone. I gripped the back of a chair, grounding myself as my wolf surged forward, all instinct and hunger.

Let me, she urged.

Not yet, I whispered back. *I need to choose.*

I met Ciaran's gaze. "You promised this wouldn't take my choice."

"It won't," he said. "But wanting doesn't mean you must act on it."

"And if I do want to?" I asked.

The bond flared—anticipation blazing through it.

Ciaran took one step closer. "Then you tell me. And I answer you knowingly."

The room narrowed. Air thickened.

I closed the distance the rest of the way.

"I want you," I said, voice steady despite everything screaming inside me. "But I don't want to lose myself."

"You won't," he said quietly. "Not if we move together."

I reached for him, hands fisting in his shirt, grounding myself in the reality of his body—his warmth, his presence anchoring the storm inside me.

The bond surged.

What followed wasn't frenzy.

It was intention strained to its limits.

Touch ignited heat. Kisses blurred into breathless need. The bond amplified every sensation until it was impossible to tell which reactions were mine and which were shared. When release came, it came hard—but it didn't erase the tension.

It only proved how thin the line had become.

After, I lay against him, breath uneven, skin too sensitive for stillness. The heat hadn't vanished—it had softened, like a wave breaking and pulling back just enough to let me breathe.

My wolf was quieter now.

Not satisfied.

But steadier.

Ciaran's hand rested at my spine. Not possessive. Not restraining. Simply there.

"This isn't over," I said.

"No," he agreed. "It rarely resolves in a single surge."

I laughed weakly. "Of course it doesn't."

The bond pulsed—warm, patient.

Outside, the sky was already beginning to darken.

And somewhere beneath the surface, something continued to gather.

Nineteen

Ciaran

I had underestimated the speed of it.

Convergence was not a gradual incline. It was acceleration—each shared moment tightening the bond, drawing it taut until there was no slack left to absorb the strain. Every breath we took in the same space, every brush of skin, every choice to remain close pushed it further along its inevitable course.

Rowan bore it with a resilience that both impressed and unsettled me.

She was not losing herself. She was choosing—again and again—to stay present inside the storm instead of letting it sweep her away. But the cost was rising. I felt it in the way her wolf pressed closer to the surface, no longer content with observation. In the way her scent shifted, deepened, sharpened—her body preparing for something it had been denied for years.

The moon was drawing nearer.

Dangerously so.

Maeve had warned me this could happen. Alignment sometimes unlocked more than intended. I had listened. I had not truly believed.

Rowan slept now, stretched across the wide couch in the sitting room, exhaustion finally claiming her. The bond was quieter—but not settled. Never settled. Before sleep had taken her, she had reached for me without opening her eyes, fingers curling into my shirt as if instinct alone knew where safety lay.

I sat beside her, pulling her carefully into my arms.

Her skin was warm—too warm—but not fevered. Power radiated from her in subtle waves, rising and falling like a tide testing its limits. I traced slow, grounding patterns along her spine, not to stir, not to claim, but to anchor.

She shifted with a soft sound, her body responding even in sleep.

“Easy,” I murmured, more to the bond than to her.

It answered with a low, restless hum.

Rowan’s wolf stirred beneath her skin, testing, pushing, retreating again. Not frantic. Not afraid.

Ready.

“She’s almost there,” Maeve said quietly from the doorway.

I did not turn. “Almost where.”

“For what she’s been holding back,” Maeve replied. “For what the bond has been stabilizing.”

I exhaled slowly. “The shift.”

Maeve nodded once. “And when it happens, Ash Valley will feel it.”

War no longer felt theoretical.

“And if she isn’t ready?” I asked.

Maeve met my gaze without softness. “Then you will have to be.”

I looked back at Rowan, something fierce and irrevocable tightening in my chest.

The bond hummed—deep, certain, unyielding.

Convergence was not ending.

It was changing form.

And when the moon rose full, Rowan would no longer be able to remain only half of what she was.

Neither would I.

Twenty

Rowan

The library was quiet in the way old places always were—heavy with memory, patient with silence.

I sat near the tall windows, a stack of books open in front of me, though I hadn't turned a page in several minutes. My attention kept slipping inward, tugged by the low, constant presence of the bond.

It wasn't urgent.

Not yet.

It felt like a held breath.

"Researching or hiding?" Maeve asked lightly.

I startled and looked up. She stood between the shelves, arms folded loosely, already dressed for the outdoors.

"Can't it be both?" I said.

Her smile softened. "Come with me."

"Where?"

"The forest," she said. "You need air. And I need to tell you something that shouldn't be said inside stone walls."

That did it.

The forest greeted us like an old friend.

Sunlight filtered through the canopy in fractured gold, the air cool and rich with earth and leaves. My wolf stirred instantly—more alert here, more present than she ever was within the castle.

Maeve noticed.

"She's closer here," she said.

"Yes," I admitted. "She always has been."

We walked for several minutes before Maeve spoke again.

"I was bonded once," she said casually.

I stopped.

She kept walking, leaving the choice with me.

I followed.

"My partner's name was Alaric," she said. "He was kind. Quiet. And devastatingly visible."

Her story unfolded without drama—only truth. A bond formed. A wolf who believed bonds were theft. An attack born of fear and resentment.

"He killed Alaric," she said simply.

The words settled like ash.

"That is why I warn," Maeve continued. "Not because bonds are dangerous. But because they make love visible. And visibility invites fear."

Understanding settled in my chest—heavy, painful, necessary.

And then—

Heat.

It bloomed suddenly, violently, low in my body. Sharp enough to steal my breath. I gasped, hands clenching at my thighs as sensation surged too fast, too intense.

Maeve was moving instantly. "Rowan."

"It's starting," I whispered. "It hurts."

The bond roared awake.

Everything sharpened—sound, scent, want. My clothes felt wrong. My skin too tight. My wolf surged forward, no longer patient, no longer restrained.

Maeve caught my arm as my knees buckled. "We're going back. Now."

Each step was agony and need tangled together, my thoughts scattering until only one remained.

Him.

Maeve half-carried me as the castle came into view, her voice steady even as my body rebelled.

"Stay with me," she commanded. "Ciaran will feel it soon."

Another wave hit as the doors opened—stronger than the last.

I clung to her, breath breaking, my wolf fully awake now and demanding release.

And with terrifying clarity, I knew—

The bond had crossed a threshold.

Whatever came next would not be gentle.

There was no turning back.

Twenty-One

Ciaran

Something was wrong.

The bond did not whisper.

It shattered.

The sensation tore through my chest with brutal force—raw, violent, unmistakable. Not arousal. Not hunger.

Alarm.

I was moving before thought formed. Power surged outward as instinct took control. Wards recoiled as I passed. Shadows bent. The castle itself seemed to recognize the urgency and yielded.

Rowan.

The pull dragged me toward the outer grounds, relentless and consuming. Control—centuries of it—slipped through my fingers like ash.

By the time I reached the courtyard, restraint was already fraying.

Maeve was there.

She had Rowan braced against her, one arm locked tight around her waist. Rowan's body trembled with waves of sensation that rolled through her unchecked—her breath broken, her eyes unfocused, her wolf pressing so close to the surface it was nearly visible.

The sight snapped something in me.

Mine.

The word was not thought. It was instinct. Command. Possession in its most dangerous form.

I was there in an instant, hands on Rowan before Maeve could speak. The bond detonated at contact—power roaring awake as Rowan turned into me with a sound that was not fear.

Relief.

Need.

Recognition.

Maeve did not release her immediately.

"Ciaran," she said sharply. "Listen to me."

I did not want to.

The world narrowed to Rowan—her scent, her heat, the way her wolf clawed against the limits of her skin. The idea of anyone else seeing her like this—touching her—sent a violent red haze through my vision.

"She's mine," I growled.

Maeve met my gaze without flinching. "Then take her. Now. Before you lose yourself completely."

That cut through just enough.

I gathered Rowan into my arms and turned for the castle, her hands fisting in my clothing, her breath hot against my throat. The bond surged again—feral, uncontained, demanding completion.

The halls blurred. Doors opened without touch. Time fractured as instinct overrode reason.

By the time I reached my chambers, restraint was no longer a choice.

The door shut.

The lock clicked.

And then the bond took over.

Not gently.

What followed was not a moment—it was a storm.

Need became language. Touch became grounding. The bond drove us together again and again, not as domination, not as surrender, but as mutual survival. Rowan met every surge with her own will, her own fire, her wolf rising to answer mine instead of being consumed by it.

Her agency was never in question.

She was not a vessel.

She was a force.

Time lost meaning. The world narrowed to convergence and collapse, to tearing apart and reassembling in the same breath.

And then—slowly—it changed.

The frantic edge dulled. The bond's scream softened into a low, resonant hum. Possessiveness remained, coiled and watchful, but no longer raging.

It was anchored.

I felt it when Rowan went still beneath me—not empty, not spent, but *whole*. Her eyes were clear when they met mine.

And beneath my hands, I felt it unmistakably.

Her wolf was no longer pressing against the surface.

It had merged.

The bond answered instantly, tightening with a final, decisive click. Chaos drained away, replaced by something vast and balanced.

Completion.

I rested my forehead against hers, both of us shaking—not from frenzy, but from the weight of what had settled into place.

The bond no longer roared.

It simply existed.

Solid. Unbreakable.

Ours.

Later—long after exhaustion finally claimed us—I felt the final shift. Not the moon.

Her.

Rowan's wolf surged fully awake, unrestrained at last. Her body recalibrated beside mine with devastating precision.

Balance.

Only then did sleep take us.

Twenty-Two

Rowan

I found him in the eastern corridor, where the windows curved outward and caught the late light just before dusk. He was still, hands clasped behind his back, gaze fixed somewhere beyond the stone as if he were listening to something only he could hear.

"Ciaran," I said.

He turned immediately. He always did now.

"You're awake," he said, relief threading through the bond before he could mask it.

"Barely," I replied. My body still felt different—settled, heavier in the best way. Like something had finally locked into place. My wolf stirred at the edge of my awareness, not restless, but alert. Curious.

I hesitated, then said, "Will you walk with me?"

His brow furrowed. "The gardens are open."

I shook my head. "Not the gardens."

Understanding sharpened his gaze. "Rowan."

"The forest," I said simply.

The bond pulsed—warm, steady—but beneath it, I felt his concern flare.

"It isn't safe," he said. "Not tonight."

"The moon?" I asked.

"Yes."

I lifted my chin. "That's exactly why."

Ciaran exhaled slowly. "You don't yet know how your body will respond."

"I know," I said. "But I also know that if I pretend nothing has changed, I'll lose something important."

My wolf pressed closer. We need this.

Ciaran's jaw tightened. "The gardens would be safer."

"I don't want safe," I said quietly. "I want honest."

Silence stretched between us.

Then he nodded once. "We stay close to the treeline."

A smile broke free before I could stop it. "Thank you."

He offered his arm. "If you run, I will catch you."

"That sounds like a challenge," I said.

The forest greeted us with quiet reverence, branches swaying gently, the air cooler and damp with moss and earth. The moon hung low, pale and watchful, its pull no longer a distant ache but a living thread tugging at my bones.

Something shifted inside me.

I stopped abruptly.

Ciaran turned at once. "Rowan?"

"I don't know what's happening," I said, breath hitching. My skin felt tight, like it didn't quite fit. My wolf stirred, pressing forward with uncharacteristic confidence.

You're ready, she said.

"For what?" I whispered.

To stop holding yourself back.

My heart pounded. "Ciaran," I said. "Something's—"

He didn't interrupt. He simply stepped closer, hands hovering but not touching. "Talk to me."

"I can feel her," I said. "Not like before. She's not asking. She's… waiting."

Ciaran's voice dropped. "Then listen to her."

The forest seemed to hush.

The sensation rolled through me—not pain, not fear—but release. My body folded inward and outward all at once, bones reshaping with startling fluidity, skin giving way to fur as the world sharpened into scent and sound and movement.

And then—

I was standing on four legs.

I blinked, breath rushing through a body that felt impossibly right. My paws pressed into the soil, grounding, real. My wolf stretched, luxuriating in the space she finally had.

Ciaran stood frozen a few feet away.

Speechless.

I tilted my head, tail flicking experimentally. *Well?*

He laughed—a soft, stunned sound. "You're magnificent."

Warmth flooded me. I took an experimental step, then another. The forest opened around me like it had been waiting.

And then I ran.

The joy was instant and overwhelming. I darted between trees, leapt over roots, the night air rushing past me in a blur of freedom.

Ciaran vanished—and reappeared ahead of me, grinning.

"Oh, that's unfair," I thought at him.

He tapped my nose lightly and vanished again.

Game on.

We ran for what felt like hours, chasing and circling, laughter and exhilaration ringing through the bond. When I finally slowed, chest heaving, thirst hit me suddenly and sharp.

I followed the sound of water to a narrow stream, clear and cold. I drank deeply, savoring the sensation, the grounding reality of it.

When I shifted back, the chill hit immediately.

I hugged myself—and froze.

Something moved at the edge of the trees.

Grey. Still. Watching.

My heart jumped.

"Ciaran," I said softly. "I thought I saw—"

He was there instantly, placing his shirt over my shoulders, guiding me gently away. "Just your senses adjusting," he said smoothly. "The forest plays tricks when everything is new."

Maybe.

But the feeling lingered.

He swept me into his arms, and the world blurred as he carried us back to the castle, speed stealing the air from my lungs.

The bath was already drawn, steam curling softly. He helped me in with careful hands, attentive, reverent. His touch was deliberate, lingering just enough to tease without crossing the line.

"You're enjoying this," I murmured.

His mouth curved. "Immensely."

He washed my hair, my shoulders, my arms—every movement slow, controlled, intimate in a way that made my skin hum.

But he never pushed.

When he finally stepped back, I was flushed and smiling and entirely undone.

"You did well," he said quietly.

My wolf purred.

And somewhere beyond the walls, unseen eyes watched the castle lights burn long into the night.

Twenty-Three

Ash Valley

The grey wolf did not slow until the forest thinned.

He crossed the boundary stones at full run, lungs burning, legs shaking as he shifted at the edge of the clearing. Skin reformed clumsily as he stumbled forward, breath tearing from his chest.

"The Alpha," he gasped.

The camp stirred immediately.

Torches flared. Wolves emerged from shadow and tent, eyes sharp, bodies tense. At the center of it all stood **Tristen**, unmoving beside the fire, power radiating from him in controlled, disciplined waves.

"You ran hard," Tristen said. Not concern. Assessment.

"I saw her," the wolf said. "On the western edge. Vampire territory."

The murmurs started instantly.

Tristen lifted a hand.

Silence fell.

"Speak," he said.

"She wasn't alone," the wolf continued. "The vampire lord was with her."

That drew attention.

"And?" Tristen asked.

"She shifted."

The word hit the clearing like a crack of thunder.

"That's not possible," someone said.

"She never could," another muttered.

Tristen's gaze never left the messenger. "Describe what you saw."

The wolf swallowed. "She didn't look like any wolf I've ever seen. Not Ash Valley. Not rogue. Her coat—" He hesitated. "It wasn't just color. It was… different. Clean. Balanced. Like the forest recognized her."

Tristen's jaw tightened almost imperceptibly.

"She was mated," the wolf added. "Bonded. Claimed."

That landed harder than the shift.

Tristen nodded once.

"That will be all," he said calmly.

Confusion flickered across faces, but no one challenged him. One by one, the pack dispersed, the fire crackling louder as the clearing emptied.

When only four remained—Tristen, his mate, the messenger, and the beta—Tristen spoke again.

"Eamon," he said.

The beta stepped forward immediately. Tall. Scarred. Quietly lethal.

"Take him to eat," Tristen ordered. "Then rest."

The grey wolf didn't argue. He bowed his head and left quickly, relief and unease warring in his expression.

When the clearing was finally empty, Tristen turned.

His mate folded her arms. "She shifted."

"Yes," Tristen said flatly.

"And bonded," Eamon added.

"Yes."

Silence stretched.

Then Tristen spoke again—lower now. Controlled. Dangerous.

"She was never supposed to survive long enough for this."

Eamon's eyes narrowed. "You're certain?"

"I was there when her parents died," Tristen said.

The words settled like ash.

His mate inhaled sharply. "You said it was a border skirmish."

"It was," Tristen replied. "One I ensured turned fatal."

Eamon didn't react outwardly, but something sharpened in his posture. "Her lineage?"

"Powerful," Tristen said. "Old. Too close to things we buried. Her mother's wolf could have rivaled an Alpha if she'd been allowed to mature. Her father knew too much."

"And the child?" Eamon asked quietly.

Tristen's gaze darkened. "I thought her broken. Unable to shift. Safe."

His mate shook her head slowly. "You were wrong."

"Yes," Tristen said. "And now she's bonded to something worse."

Eamon's jaw clenched. "A vampire prince."

"One with power," Tristen agreed. "And territory. And protection."

"And if she realizes what she is," his mate said, voice tight, "she won't be vulnerable for long."

Tristen turned to Eamon fully now.

"You will go," he said. "Verify what was seen."

Eamon nodded once. "And if it's true?"

Tristen didn't hesitate.

"Then she dies."

"And the vampire?" Eamon asked.

"That is a complication," Tristen said. "Not a deterrent."

His mate stepped closer. "We should have killed her as a child."

"No," Tristen said. "That would have drawn attention. This was cleaner."

He looked toward the dark forest beyond their borders.

"But we move now," he continued. "Before she understands her power. Before the bond finishes reshaping her."

Eamon bowed his head. "I'll leave before dawn."

"Good," Tristen said.

The fire crackled, sending sparks into the night.

"She was never meant to come into herself," Tristen said quietly. "Her bloodline nearly cost us everything once."

And this time, he would not leave it unfinished.

Twenty-Four

Ciaran

The court assembled because I summoned them.

That alone shifted the balance.

They gathered in the High Hall beneath vaulted stone and ancestral banners, their voices low, expressions carefully neutral. Elders, advisors, bloodbound lords—those who had served my father, and those who had waited patiently for the moment when patience would no longer be required.

They felt it.

The bond.

Even restrained, even settled, it radiated authority in a way no title ever had.

I stood at the head of the chamber, hands clasped behind my back, posture composed. No crown. No ceremony. None of it was necessary.

"Speak," I said.

Silence stretched.

Finally, Lord Varyn stepped forward—old, silver-eyed, clever enough to be dangerous and careful enough to survive it.

"The bond has sealed," he said. Not a question.

"Yes."

Murmurs rippled through the hall.

"And the convergence," Lady Sereth added. "It lasted longer than expected."

"A week," another voice said. "That alone—"

I lifted one hand.

The room stilled immediately.

"The bond is sealed," I repeated. "That is all you are entitled to know without permission."

A calculated risk. One that paid off in sharpened attention.

Varyn inclined his head slightly. "Tradition dictates—"

"I am aware of tradition," I cut in. "I am also aware of what happens when tradition mistakes entitlement for authority."

That landed.

Several faces tightened.

"You will not pressure her," I continued, voice calm, controlled, lethal in its certainty. "Not directly. Not indirectly. Not through rumor, suggestion, or manufactured concern."

"And if the court believes delay threatens stability?" Sereth asked.

I turned my gaze to her fully. "Then the court should concern itself with *why* stability would shatter without immediate possession of a woman who has been here less than a month."

That drew a sharp intake of breath from somewhere behind her.

"She is not property," I went on. "She is not leverage. She is not a symbol to be deployed for your comfort."

"And yet," Varyn said carefully, "once married, you ascend."

Yes.

There it was.

The truth they all circled.

"As king," he continued, "your authority would be unquestioned. Your rule—secured."

"I do not require a wife to rule," I said evenly.

"But the realm—"

"Will adapt," I snapped. The sound cracked like stone under strain. "Or it will learn the cost of refusing to."

The bond stirred in response, not flaring—*confirming*.

They felt it. I saw it in the way several of them shifted, instinct recognizing dominance long before politics could justify it.

"The delay," Sereth pressed, regrouping, "how long do you intend to push ceremony?"

"As long as she needs," I said. "Six months, if necessary."

That broke the room open.

Voices rose—controlled, but urgent.

"Six months invites speculation."

"Six months weakens perception."

"Six months gives enemies room."

I let them speak.

Then—

"It is not negotiable."

Silence fell again, heavier this time.

Varyn studied me for a long moment. "And if she decides not to marry you at all?"

The question was not concern.

It was a test.

"Then I remain bonded," I said. "And the realm survives."

Several elders stiffened.

"That is… unprecedented."

"So was sealing a bond without coercion," I replied. "We are clearly in a period of adjustment."

Sereth hesitated, then said, "There is another concern."

I already knew what it would be.

"Heirs," she said.

The word echoed unpleasantly in the vaulted hall.

"You are assuming facts not in evidence," I said coolly.

"The convergence lasted a week," another elder said. "Such intensity—such alignment—traditionally—"

"Tradition does not account for *this* bond," I interrupted. "Nor this pairing."

A pause.

Then Varyn asked the question they all wanted answered.

"Is it even possible," he said slowly, "for a vampire and a werewolf to conceive?"

I did not answer immediately.

Because the truth was uncomfortable.

"Rare," I said at last. "But not impossible."

The room shifted.

"And after convergence," Sereth pressed, "how can we know she is not already—"

"You won't," I said flatly.

That silenced them.

"She will not be examined," I continued. "She will not be speculated about. And her body will not become a topic of court discussion."

Varyn's eyes sharpened. "If an heir exists—"

"—then you will learn of it when *she* chooses to share that knowledge," I said, power threading every word. "Not before."

"And if she is not with child?" another asked.

"Then nothing changes," I replied. "Because my rule does not hinge on her womb."

That was the line.

The one that drew real fear.

Because they all understood what it meant.

I stepped forward, letting the bond breathe just enough to remind them who stood before them.

"You are not wrong to think of the future," I said. "But you are wrong to believe you control it."

My gaze swept the hall.

"She will not be rushed."

"She will not be cornered."

"And she will not be sacrificed to soothe your anxieties."

I paused, letting the weight of it settle.

"If you cannot accept that," I finished quietly, "then you should reconsider your place in my court."

No one spoke.

When I turned and left, the hall parted without a word.

And as the doors closed behind me, the bond answered—not with hunger, not with urgency—

But with certainty.

Whatever crown awaited me would come later.

What mattered now was this:

No one would ever make Rowan feel like a price paid for power.

Not while I drew breath.

Twenty-Five

Rowan

I learned the court did not push all at once.

It nudged.

Soft words. Polite concern. Smiles that lingered a fraction too long. Questions that weren't questions at all.

"How are you settling?"

"You must be exhausted after… everything."

"If there's anything you need, truly—"

Always followed by a glance.

At my hands.

My posture.

My body.

At first, I told myself I was imagining it.

Ciaran said the bond sharpened perception. That my senses were still calibrating. That not every look meant intent.

But my wolf noticed.

She bristled when certain courtiers entered a room. She paced when servants lingered too close. She pressed forward when voices dropped around corners.

Something wasn't right.

I was standing near one of the eastern balconies when Lady Sereth approached again—graceful, silver-haired, impeccably calm.

"You should be taking supplements," she said conversationally, handing me a small glass vial filled with pale liquid. "The convergence can leave... deficits."

I stared at it.

"It's just a tonic," she added smoothly. "We give it to all bonded consorts. Vitamins, really."

Consorts.

The word scraped.

"I didn't ask for one," I said.

She smiled. "Of course not. But the body doesn't always wait for permission."

My wolf growled.

Low. Internal. Warning.

Before I could respond, Maeve's hand closed around my wrist.

Firm. Immediate.

"No," Maeve said flatly.

Lady Sereth's smile froze.

"That isn't for her," Maeve continued, eyes hard now. "And you know it."

The air shifted.

"What are you implying?" Sereth asked coolly.

"That potion prevents conception," Maeve replied. "And that giving it without consent would be... unwise."

Silence snapped tight.

I felt it then—the truth clicking into place with sickening clarity.

They weren't worried about me.

They were managing me.

I pulled my hand back slowly.

"Is this how your court treats guests?" I asked.

Sereth's expression cooled. "You misunderstand—"

"No," I said, voice steady despite the heat rising in my chest. "I don't."

Maeve stepped between us. "Leave."

Sereth hesitated—then inclined her head stiffly and walked away.

I stared at the vial still clutched in my palm.

"This happens often?" I asked quietly.

Maeve met my gaze. "Only when power is nervous."

My wolf snarled approval.

Ciaran found me later that night in the upper sitting room, pacing barefoot across the stone floor.

"You're angry," he said gently.

"I was almost drugged," I replied.

His control cracked.

Not visibly. Not explosively.

But the bond tightened—sharp, lethal, furious.

He crossed the room in two strides and took my hands, grounding himself against me as much as anchoring me.

"I'm sorry," he said. "I warned them. Apparently not clearly enough."

"They were trying to decide something for me," I said. "Again."

His jaw clenched. "Never again."

I studied his face. "What were they afraid of?"

He didn't answer immediately.

That told me everything.

"Ciaran," I said softly. "Talk to me."

He exhaled slowly and guided me to the couch, sitting beside me—close, but not crowding.

"The bond," he said carefully. "Now that it's sealed, it includes more than sensation and power."

I waited.

"Our thoughts brush," he continued. "Our instincts align. And in rare cases… so do bloodlines."

I felt my breath catch.

"They're worried about children," I said.

"Yes."

"With me," I added.

"Yes."

The word landed heavier than I expected.

"Is it possible?" I asked quietly.

He nodded once. "Rare. Unpredictable. And not something anyone has the right to control."

I stared at my hands.

"My body isn't a political problem," I said.

"No," he said fiercely. "It's yours."

"And if I were already pregnant?" I asked.

His gaze softened. "Then that would be *your* truth to share. Or not."

The bond warmed—steady, reassuring.

"I don't even know if I want that," I admitted. "Not yet. I barely know who I am with all of this."

"That's why I delayed the wedding," he said. "Six months was the most the court would tolerate without open rebellion."

"And you?" I asked. "What do you want?"

He met my eyes without flinching.

"I want you to choose me," he said. "Not a crown. Not a future you didn't consent to. *Me.*"

My wolf eased for the first time all day.

I leaned into him, resting my forehead against his chest.

"They won't stop," I murmured.

"No," he agreed. "They'll test. They always do."

"Then I need to learn how to push back," I said.

A slow smile curved his mouth.

"You already are."

Outside, the castle settled into uneasy quiet.

And somewhere beyond the walls, plans were already shifting.

But this time—

I knew the danger wasn't just out there.

It was inside the halls.

Watching.

Waiting.

Twenty-Six

Maeve

I had known they would test him.

What I had not known—what chilled me even now—was how quickly they had decided to test *her* instead.

Ciaran listened without interrupting.

That alone told me how angry he was.

I stood across from him in the private council chamber, the vial resting between us on the table like a confession that had learned to glow. Pale liquid. Harmless-looking. Carefully prepared.

"Lady Sereth," I said. "And two others. One from the eastern bloodlines, one who serves under the old fertility rites. They did not coordinate openly, but they didn't need to. The court remembers its habits."

Ciaran's fingers curled slowly against the stone.

"They offered it as a supplement," I continued. "Something to 'support recovery.' If Rowan had taken it for even three days—"

"I know what it does," he said quietly.

That was worse than fury.

That was control sharpened to a blade.

He picked up the vial, examined it once, then closed his hand around it hard enough that the glass cracked.

"Who authorized it?" he asked.

"No one," I replied. "Which means everyone."

Silence pressed in.

"This used to be a shared position," I said, not accusing. Simply stating. "When Alaric lived, they never would have dared move without consensus. Without permission."

Ciaran's jaw tightened. "They mistook restraint for absence."

"They mistook *me* for a relic," I said.

He finally looked at me then. Really looked.

"I want them punished," he said.

"Of course."

"No," he corrected. "I want them *seen*."

That familiar, dangerous clarity slid into place—the one that reminded the court exactly why they feared him.

"Strip them of privacy," he continued. "Of dignity. Of the illusion that this was a quiet correction instead of a violation."

I inclined my head. "Public?"

"The Great Hall," he said. "At dawn."

He slid the vial back across the table toward me.

"Place it with their names," he added. "Let the court understand precisely what was almost done. And why I warned them not to touch her."

My chest tightened—not with fear, but with something older.

Pride.

"Yes, my prince," I said.

He stopped me before I reached the door.

"And Maeve," he said softly.

I turned.

"Thank you," he said. "For catching it."

I nodded once and left before the memories could catch me too.

The corridors were quieter than they should have been.

Whispers followed me like drafts through cracked doors. Servants avoided my gaze. Courtiers pretended not to see me as I passed.

Good.

Let them remember what vigilance looked like.

As I worked—issuing summons, sealing records, ordering guards whose loyalty I trusted—I felt the old ache stir. The one that never truly slept.

Alaric would have stood beside me for this.

He would have cataloged every fracture while I read the emotional currents. He would have teased me for being too merciful, then quietly doubled the consequences when he thought I wasn't looking.

We had balanced each other.

The way bonds were meant to.

Now I balanced alone.

I paused briefly at the window overlooking the inner courtyard, the moon pale above the towers.

"You would have liked her," I murmured to no one. "She's stubborn. Unafraid. Dangerous in all the right ways."

The castle creaked softly around me, as if listening.

By the time dawn neared, the fractures were exposed.

Three houses fractured inward, scrambling to distance themselves. Two others closed ranks too tightly—guilty by silence if not action. Old loyalties resurfaced. Old grudges sharpened.

Good.

Rot only spreads when it stays hidden.

I arranged the display myself.

The tonic vial—intact now, carefully restored—sat on a black velvet cushion. Beside it, three names. No embellishment. No explanation.

The truth rarely needed either.

As the Great Hall filled, I stood at the edge and watched realization spread.

Fear.

Outrage.

And beneath it all—

Understanding.

Ciaran entered last.

The room stilled instantly.

I did not envy the court their morning.

And as I finally allowed myself to sit—eyes burning, bones heavy from a night without rest—I accepted the truth I had been circling since Rowan crossed our threshold.

The court was breaking.

But not because of her.

Because she had exposed how fragile their control truly was.

And this time—

We would not let it reform in secret.

Twenty-Seven

Rowan

The court didn't explode.

That would have been honest.

It did something worse.

It adapted.

By midday, the Great Hall had returned to its polished rhythm. Servants moved as if nothing had happened. Courtiers spoke in careful tones. Faces were composed.

But eyes lingered.

Not openly.

Not long enough to call it staring.

Just long enough to feel like a hand at the back of my neck.

I learned quickly what Maeve meant by *fractures.*

A fracture wasn't always a break.

Sometimes it was a hairline crack you only saw when the light hit right.

I caught it in the way House Neryth suddenly praised me too loudly.

In the way House Vaelor refused to meet my gaze at all.

In the way certain servants avoided touching my cup.

As if I might bite.

My wolf bared her teeth internally.

Let them be afraid, she said.

"I'm trying," I muttered under my breath, "to be civilized."

Boring.

I was in the east gallery when Maeve found me.

Not looking for me.

Just…appearing. Like a shadow that had decided it belonged here.

"You're pacing," she observed.

"I'm walking," I corrected.

Maeve's mouth twitched. "You're walking a hole into the stone."

I stopped near a window and stared out at the forest beyond the walls.

It looked the same as always.

It didn't feel the same.

My senses kept catching on details I couldn't name.

A shift in wind.

A bird going silent.

A stretch of shadow that felt too still.

Maeve stepped closer without crowding.

"Your wolf is listening," she said.

"She's been listening," I replied. "I'm the one who's behind."

Maeve's gaze flicked over me. Not judgmental.

Assessing.

"Do you want to learn how to move through them?" she asked.

"The courtiers?"

"Yes."

I blew out a breath. "I don't want to move through them at all."

"Then you'll always feel like prey," Maeve said simply. "Even when you aren't."

That landed.

Not like an insult.

Like a truth I hadn't wanted to admit.

I turned my head slightly. "So what. Etiquette lessons?"

Maeve looked mildly offended.

"Politics," she corrected. "There's a difference."

My mouth curved. "I'm thrilled."

Maeve ignored that. "Come."

"Where?"

"Anywhere that isn't a window," she said. "The court is learning. So are you. But you can't do it while you're half inside the forest."

I hesitated.

Then followed.

We moved through corridors that didn't feel like corridors so much as… channels. Places where power flowed. Where ears waited behind stone.

Maeve's pace was unhurried. Controlled.

I copied it.

It took effort.

When we reached a smaller hall lined with portraits, Maeve stopped.

"You're still thinking like a guest," she said.

"I am a guest."

Maeve's eyes sharpened. "No."

My wolf lifted her head.

Maeve gestured toward the paintings—ancient faces in velvet and blood-red silk.

"Guests are tolerated," she said. "You are *bonded.* That makes you permanent in a way the court can't undo."

My stomach tightened.

"Which," Maeve continued, voice cool, "means they'll stop trying to move you and start trying to move the world around you."

I swallowed.

"And how do I stop that?" I asked.

Maeve's smile was thin and almost kind.

"You don't stop it," she said. "You learn to see it. Then you decide what you allow."

My wolf purred, pleased.

Finally.

I met Maeve's gaze. "And if they don't like what I allow?"

Maeve's expression didn't change.

“Then they learn,” she said, “what it costs to mistake you for something manageable.”

Twenty-Eight

Ciaran

By evening, the castle had returned to its oldest habit.

Pretending nothing was wrong.

That was how courts survived.

Not by being loyal.

By being durable.

I stood in the private war room with three people I trusted:

Maeve.

Captain Rains, who guarded the inner halls and didn't gossip.

And Kael, who handled the wards and spoke only when his words mattered.

Kael pointed at the map with one ink-stained finger. "The western boundary stones were disturbed. Slightly."

"By animals?" Rains asked.

Kael's gaze was flat. "No."

Maeve didn't react outwardly, but I felt her attention sharpen.

I turned my head. "Ash Valley."

Maeve's mouth tightened. "Scouts."

Rains shifted, hand flexing near the hilt of his blade. "Inside our territory?"

"Close enough to test," Maeve said.

I stared at the map for a moment longer than necessary.

Not because I didn't understand.

Because I did.

They were moving.

Not with a full force.

Not yet.

With intention.

"What did they see?" Rains asked quietly.

I didn't answer immediately.

Because saying it aloud made it real.

"Her shift," Maeve said for me.

Rains went still. "That will change everything."

"Yes," I said. "It already has."

Kael cleared his throat. "The wards can be reinforced along the treeline. But there's another issue."

I looked at him.

Kael hesitated, then placed a second marker on the map.

Inside the castle walls.

Maeve's gaze snapped to it.

Rains' voice went low. "That's...inside."

"Yes," Kael said.

My control didn't crack.

It tightened.

"Explain," I said.

Kael's fingers tapped the marker once. "Something brushed the inner wards last night. Not enough to break them. Enough to test their response."

Maeve's expression cooled. "Someone inside touched them."

Rains' jaw clenched. "A traitor."

A word humans used when betrayal had to be simplified.

Courts were rarely that clean.

I exhaled slowly.

"Find who," I said to Kael.

Kael nodded once. "I will."

I turned to Rains. "Increase the guard rotation. Silent shifts. No patterns."

Rains nodded. "Yes, my prince."

Then I looked at Maeve.

Her face was calm.

Her eyes were not.

"Do not let Rowan feel caged," I said.

Maeve's mouth curved faintly. "I know."

I held her gaze. "And Maeve—"

Her eyes lifted.

"If this becomes war," I said quietly, "I want her trained before she has to learn in blood."

Maeve's expression softened a fraction. "Then she needs time in the forest."

"I know," I said.

"And she needs to stop thinking of herself as a guest," Maeve added.

My throat tightened with something that wasn't fear.

Agreement.

"She's learning," I said. "But the world will not wait."

Maeve's eyes sharpened again. "Then we make the world pay for rushing her."

Twenty-Nine

Maeve

There are two kinds of danger.

The kind that arrives with teeth.

And the kind that arrives with manners.

The castle was full of the second kind.

I moved through it quietly, letting them forget I was listening.

A maid in the south corridor paused too long outside the wrong door.

A steward carried a message that wasn't sealed.

A courtier laughed a fraction too loudly after mentioning the western woods.

Small things.

Always small.

That was how rot spread.

When I reached the servants' stairwell, I stopped long enough to watch a pair of guards change posts.

Their movements weren't wrong.

But their timing was.

A rhythm too practiced.

Like someone had told them when to look away.

I waited until the corridor was empty, then stepped into the shadowed alcove beside the tapestries.

The stone there was colder.

Old.

Listening.

"Show me," I murmured, and let my senses extend—not magic, not exactly.

Experience.

The castle answered.

Not in words.

In absence.

In the places where sound should have been but wasn't.

In the places where a corridor felt…hollow.

I followed that hollowness down to the western service door.

And there it was again.

The yew marker.

A small sprig laid as if by accident.

As if the wind had dropped it.

But yew did not grow near that door.

I did not touch it.

I stared until memory rose like a ghost.

A clearing.

A fire.

Wolves who thought border stones meant ownership.

Alaric's hand in mine.

His laughter when I took everything too seriously.

Then his blood in my mouth and the world ending in a soundless scream.

I inhaled slowly and made myself come back.

Now was not then.

Rowan was not Alaric.

But the pattern was familiar.

Visibility.

Bonds.

Envy that turned to fear.

Fear that turned to violence.

I turned from the sprig and walked back toward the central hall, mind already arranging the pieces.

Ash Valley's scouts were not the only ones watching.

Someone inside wanted the scouts to see.

Someone wanted movement.

Chaos.

Pressure.

I reached the private council chamber and found Ciaran there, alone, staring at the fire like it had personally offended him.

He looked up.

His gaze read my face instantly.

"You found something," he said.

I nodded once. "A marker."

His eyes darkened. "Inside."

"Yes."

Silence stretched.

Then I said the thing neither of us wanted to make real.

"Someone wants Ash Valley to come," I said.

Ciaran's voice went very quiet. "Why."

"To force your hand," I replied. "To force hers. To force a decision before the bond has settled into something the court can't manipulate."

His jaw tightened.

"And if they think conflict will make her break," I added, "they're wrong."

Ciaran's eyes lifted. "But they'll try anyway."

"Yes," I said.

He leaned back slightly, control still tight, but something dangerous stirring beneath it.

"Set a trap," he said.

I didn't smile.

But I felt the old, cold clarity slide into place.

"Gladly," I replied.

Thirty

Ash Valley

Eamon did not dream.

Dreams were for wolves who still believed the world cared what they wanted.

He woke before dawn, dressed without sound, and stepped into the cold with the same calm he used before killing.

The camp was quiet.

Too quiet.

Tristen stood at the edge of the clearing, arms folded, the fire reduced to embers.

He didn't look at Eamon when he spoke.

"You will not be seen," Tristen said.

Eamon inclined his head. "Of course."

"And you will not engage," Tristen added.

Eamon's gaze lifted. "Unless necessary."

Tristen's mouth tightened. "Unless ordered."

A thin thread of tension ran between them—respect, yes.

But also warning.

Tristen finally turned his head slightly. "If she is what the scout described…"

Eamon said nothing.

Tristen's voice dropped. "Then she is a threat."

Eamon's eyes sharpened. "Or a key."

Tristen's gaze flickered—annoyance, quickly controlled.

"Do not romanticize this," Tristen said. "Her bloodline nearly cost us everything once."

Eamon nodded once, though he didn't like being reminded that Tristen's sins were considered *strategy.*

He stepped back. "I'll verify."

Tristen's mate appeared from the shadow of a tent, her expression unreadable.

"Bring certainty," she said.

Eamon held her gaze. "I always do."

He left before the sun broke the horizon.

The forest accepted him like it accepted all predators—without judgment.

Hours later, the boundary stones came into view.

Vampire territory.

The air changed.

Not colder.

Heavier.

Warded.

Eamon slowed, eyes narrowing as he watched the treeline.

He didn't cross.

Not yet.

He listened.

And somewhere beyond stone walls and old magic, he felt it.

A pulse.

Not moon-driven.

Not pack.

Something…balanced.

Something that did not belong to either side.

Eamon's mouth tightened.

"So it's true," he murmured.

And then, carefully, he stepped closer.

Thirty-One

Rowan

That night, the castle felt like it was pretending.

Like a house that smiled while it listened for footsteps outside the door.

The moon hung low and pale.

Not full.

Not yet.

But close enough to tug at my bones.

I found Ciaran on the western battlement, hands clasped behind his back, gaze fixed on the forest like he was daring it to blink first.

I leaned on the stone beside him. "You look dramatic."

His eyes flicked to me. "I look alert."

"Same thing," I said.

His mouth curved faintly, but the bond stayed tight—watchful.

"Maeve thinks someone inside is feeding information," I said.

Ciaran didn't deny it.

That alone made my wolf rise.

Finally, she said. *Something worth biting.*

"Not helping," I muttered.

Ciaran's gaze slid to me. "Talk to me."

I exhaled slowly and stared out at the trees.

"I don't like being watched," I said. "I know that sounds…obvious."

"It doesn't," he replied.

"It should," I said dryly.

Ciaran's hand brushed mine on the stone. Not a grip.

An offer.

I took it.

"I can handle the court staring," I continued. "I can handle their whispers. I can handle their…polite little tests."

My wolf snarled agreement.

"But this," I said, nodding toward the forest, "feels different."

Ciaran's voice lowered. "Because it is."

I glanced at him. "Tell me the truth."

His eyes held mine.

"Ash Valley has scouts near the boundary," he said. "And there was a brush against the inner wards."

My stomach tightened.

"Inside," I repeated.

"Yes."

I looked back at the forest and felt the world sharpen.

Not fear.

Focus.

I didn't realize I'd been waiting my whole life to feel that.

"Okay," I said.

Ciaran's brow furrowed. "That's all?"

I lifted a shoulder. "Do you want me to panic? I can try if it'll make you feel useful."

A surprised exhale—almost a laugh—slipped out of him.

My wolf purred.

Good. Keep him off balance.

"You're unbearable," Ciaran murmured.

"Mm," I said, pleased. "And yet you bonded me anyway."

His gaze warmed briefly, then darkened again with the weight behind it.

"Rowan," he said quietly, "if something comes through that treeline—"

"I won't be hidden," I cut in.

Ciaran's jaw tightened.

I held his gaze. "I won't be reckless either. But I am done being treated like I'm made of glass."

His hand lifted, stopping just short of my cheek.

"May I?" he asked.

I nodded.

His palm cupped my face gently.

The bond steadied.

Held.

"You're not glass," he said.

"I know."

His thumb brushed my cheek once. "Then what are you."

I stared at him for a beat, then answered honestly.

"New," I said. "And dangerous."

A faint smile touched his mouth. "Yes."

Below us, the forest swayed.

And for a moment, I felt it—something at the edge of my senses.

Not sound.

Not scent.

Attention.

My wolf went still.

There, she whispered.

I didn't move. I didn't react.

I only breathed.

Ciaran's posture shifted subtly, power tightening in his frame like a drawn blade.

"You feel it," he said.

"Yes," I whispered.

The presence didn't come closer.

It didn't retreat either.

Just…watched.

I leaned in slightly, mouth near Ciaran's ear.

"If I run," I murmured, "will you catch me?"

His breath hitched—just once.

"Yes," he said. Immediate.

I smiled, small and sharp.

"Good," I replied. "Because I'm not running away."

The bond pulsed—warm, steady, and utterly unafraid.

And somewhere in the trees, the watcher finally shifted.

Not leaving.

Just repositioning.

Like this was only the beginning.

www.ingramcontent.com/pod-product-compliance
Lightning Source LLC
LaVergne TN
LVHW090530110826
845146LV00003B/1039